'You... would imply that I feared. Darcy's mouth barely moved as she spoke. 'And I don't. At least, not about you—o... our bab...'

Her fingers flu... ...d over the swell of her belly and Renzo's heart gave a sudden leap as he allowed his gaze to rest on it. 'I am prepared to support you both.' His voice thickened and deepened. 'But on one condition.'

'Let me guess. Sole custody for you, I suppose? With the occasional access visit for me, probably accompanied by some ghastly nanny of your choice?'

'I'm hoping it won't come to that,' he said evenly. 'But I will not have a Sabatini heir growing up illegitimately.'

He walked over to the window and stared out at the heavy winter clouds before turning back again.

'This child stands to inherit my empire, but only if he or she bears my name. So, yes, I will support you, Darcy—but it will be on my terms. And the first non-negotiable one is that you marry me.'

One Night With Consequences

When one night...leads to pregnancy!

When succumbing to a night of unbridled desire
it's impossible to think past the morning after!

But, with the sheets barely settled, that little blue line
appears on the pregnancy test and it doesn't take long
to realise that one night of white-hot passion
has turned into a lifetime of consequences!

Only one question remains:

How do you tell a man you've just met
that you're about to share more than just his bed?

Find out in:

The Shock Cassano Baby by Andie Brock

An Heir to Make a Marriage by Abby Green

The Greek's Nine-Month Redemption by Maisey Yates

Crowned for the Prince's Heir by Sharon Kendrick

The Sheikh's Baby Scandal by Carol Marinelli

A Ring for Vincenzo's Heir by Jennie Lucas

Claiming His Christmas Consequence by Michelle Smart

The Guardian's Virgin Ward by Caitlin Crews

A Child Claimed by Gold by Rachael Thomas

The Consequence of His Vengeance by Jennie Lucas

Look for more **One Night With Consequences**
coming soon!

SECRETS OF A BILLIONAIRE'S MISTRESS

BY
SHARON KENDRICK

First Published in Great Britain 2017
By Mills & Boon, an imprint of HarperCollins*Publishers*
1 London Bridge Street, London, SE1 9GF

© 2017 Sharon Kendrick

ISBN: 978-0-263-92403-9

Printed and bound in Spain
by CPI, Barcelona

Sharon Kendrick once won a national writing competition by describing her ideal date: being flown to an exotic island by a gorgeous and powerful man. Little did she realise that she'd just wandered into her dream job! Today she writes for Mills & Boon, featuring often stubborn but always *to die for* heroes and the women who bring them to their knees. She believes that the best books are those you never want to end. Just like life…

Books by Sharon Kendrick

Mills & Boon Modern Romance

A Royal Vow of Convenience
The Ruthless Greek's Return
Christmas in Da Conti's Bed
The Greek's Marriage Bargain
A Scandal, a Secret, a Baby
The Sheikh's Undoing
Monarch of the Sands
Too Proud to be Bought

The Billionaire's Legacy

Di Sione's Virgin Mistress

The Bond of Billionaires

Claimed for Makarov's Baby
The Sheikh's Christmas Conquest

One Night With Consequences

Carrying the Greek's Heir
Crowned for the Prince's Heir

Wedlocked!

The Billionaire's Defiant Acquisition

Visit the Author Profile page
at millsandboon.co.uk for more titles.

For three fabulous writers who helped with the
Australian detail in my 100th book,
A Royal Vow of Convenience.

Helene Young and Margareta Young,
for the inspiration and the insight—
and Rachael Johns, for the Tim-Tams!

CHAPTER ONE

RENZO SABATINI WAS unbuttoning his shirt when the doorbell rang. He felt the beat of expectation. The familiar tug of heat to his groin. He was half-tempted to pull the shirt from his shoulders so Darcy could slide her fingers over his skin, closely followed by those inventive lips of hers. The soft lick of her tongue could help him forget what lay ahead. He thought about Tuscany and the closing of a chapter. About the way some memories could still be raw even when so many years had passed and maybe that was why he never really stopped to think about them.

But why concentrate on darkness when Darcy was all sunshine and light? And why rush at sex when they had the whole night ahead—a smorgasbord of sensuality which he could enjoy at his leisure with his latest and most unexpected lover? A woman who demanded nothing other than that he satisfy her—something which was easy since he had only to touch her pale skin to grow so hard that it hurt. His mouth dried. Four months in and he was as bewitched by her as he had been from the start.

In many ways he was astonished it had continued this long when their two worlds were so different. She was not his usual type of woman and he was very definitely not her type of man. He was into clean lines and minimalism, while Darcy was all voluptuous curves and lingerie which could barely contain her abundant flesh. His mouth curved into a hard smile. In reality it should never have lasted beyond one night but her tight body had been difficult to walk away from. It still was.

The doorbell rang again and the glance he shot at his wristwatch was touched with irritation. Was she daring to be *impatient* when she wasn't supposed to be here for another half hour? Surely she knew the rules by now...that she was expected to fit around his schedule, rather than the other way round?

Barefooted, he walked through the spacious rooms of his Belgravia apartment, pulling open the front door to see Darcy Denton standing there—small of stature and impossible to ignore—her magnificent curls misted with rain and tugged back into a ponytail so that only the bright red colour was on show. She wore a light raincoat, tightly belted to emphasise her tiny waist, but underneath she was still in her waitress's uniform because she lived on the other side of London, an area Renzo had never visited—and he was perfectly content for it to stay that way. They'd established very quickly that if she went home after her shift to change, it wasted several hours—even if he sent his car to collect her. And Renzo was a busy man with an architectural practice which spanned several continents. His time was too precious to waste, which was why she always came straight from work with her overnight bag—though that was a largely unnecessary detail since she was rarely anything other than naked when she was with him.

He stared down into her green eyes, which glittered like emeralds in porcelain-pale skin and, as always, his blood began to fizz with expectation and lust. 'You're early,' he observed softly. 'Did you time your visit especially because you knew I'd be undressing?'

Darcy answered him with a tight smile as he opened the door to let her in. She was cold and she was wet and it had been the most awful day. A customer had spilt tea over her uniform. Then a child had been sick. She'd looked out the window at the end of her shift to discover that the rain had started and someone must have taken her umbrella. And Renzo Sabatini was standing there in the warmth of his palatial apartment, looking glowing and delectable—making the assumption that she had nothing better to do than to time her visits just so she would find him half-naked. Could she ever have met a man more arrogant?

Yet she'd known what she was letting herself in for when she'd started this crazy affair. When she'd fought a silent battle against everything she'd known to be wrong. Because powerful men who dallied with waitresses only wanted one thing, didn't they?

She'd lost that particular battle and ended up in Renzo's king-size bed—but nobody could say that her eyes hadn't been open at the time. Well, some of the time at least—the rest of the time they'd fluttered to a quivering close as he had thrust deeply inside her until she was sobbing with pleasure. After resisting him as hard as she could, she'd decided to resist no more. Or maybe the truth was that she hadn't been able to stop herself from falling into his arms. He'd kissed her and that had been it. She hadn't known that a kiss could make you feel that way. She hadn't realised that desire could make you feel as if you were floating. Or flying. She'd surrendered her virginity to him and, after his shocked reaction to discovering he was her first lover, he had introduced her to more pleasure than she'd thought possible, though in a life spectacularly short on the pleasure front that wouldn't have been difficult, would it?

For a while things had been fine. More than fine. She spent the night with him whenever he was in the country and had a space in his diary—and sometimes she spent the following day there, too. He cooked her eggs and played her music she'd never heard before— dreamy stuff featuring lots of violins—while he pored over the fabulously intricate drawings which would one day be transformed into the glittering and iconic skyscrapers for which he was famous.

But lately something had started to niggle away inside her. Was it her conscience? Her sense that her already precarious self-worth was being eroded by him hiding her away in his palatial apartment, like a guilty secret? She wasn't sure. All she knew was that she'd started to analyse what she'd become and hadn't liked the answer she'd come up with.

She was a wealthy man's plaything. A woman who dropped her panties whenever he clicked those elegant olive fingers.

But she was here now and it was stupid to let her reservations spoil the evening ahead, so she changed her tight smile into a bright smile as she dumped her overnight bag on the floor and tugged the elastic band from her hair. Shaking her damp curls free, she couldn't deny the satisfaction it gave her to see the way Renzo's eyes had darkened in response—although her physical appeal to him had never been in any question. He couldn't seem to get enough of her and she suspected she knew why. Because she was different. Working class, for a start. She hadn't been to college—in fact, she'd missed out on more schooling than she should have done and nearly everything she knew had been self-taught. She was curvy and red-headed, when usually he went for slender brunettes—that was if all the photos in the newspapers were to be believed. They were certainly mismatched on just about every level, except when it came to bed.

Because the sex was amazing—it always had been—but it couldn't continue like this, taking her on an aimless path which was leading nowhere. Darcy knew what she had to do. She knew you could only fool yourself for so long before reality started hurting and forced you to change. She'd noticed Renzo was starting to take her for granted and knew that, if it continued, all the magic they'd shared would just wither away. And she didn't want that, because memories were powerful things. The bad ones were like heavy burdens you had to carry around with you and she was determined to have some good ones to lighten the load. So when was she going to grab the courage to walk away from him, before Renzo did the walking and left her feeling broken and crushed?

'I'm early because I sent your driver away and took the Tube instead,' she explained, brushing excess raindrops from her forest of red curls.

'You sent the driver away?' He frowned as he slid the damp raincoat from her shoulders. 'Why on earth would you do that?'

Darcy sighed, wondering what it must be like to be Renzo Sabatini and live in an enclosed and protected world, where chauffeur-driven cars and private jets shielded you from rain and snow and the worries of most normal folk. Where people did your shopping and picked up your clothes where you'd left them on the bedroom floor the night before. A world where you didn't have to speak to anyone unless you really wanted to, because there was always some minion who would do the speaking for you.

'Because the traffic is a nightmare at this time of day and often we're forced to sit in a queue, moving at a snail's pace.' She took the coat from him and gave it a little shake before hanging it in the cupboard. 'Public transport happens to have a lot going for it during the rush hour. Now, rather than debating my poor timekeeping can I please have a cup of tea? I'm f-f-freezing.'

But he didn't make any move towards the kitchen as most people might have done after such a wobbly request. He took her in his arms and kissed her instead. His lips were hard as they pressed against hers and his fingers caressed her bottom through her uniform dress as he brought her up close to his body. Close enough for her to feel the hardness of his erection and the warmth of his bare chest as he deepened the kiss. Darcy's eyelids fluttered to a close as one hard thigh pushed insistently against hers and she could feel her own parting in automatic response. And suddenly her coldness was forgotten and tea was the last thing on her mind. Her questions and insecurities dissolved as he deepened the kiss and all she was aware of was the building heat as her chilled fingers crept up to splay themselves over his bare and hair-roughened torso.

'Hell, Renzo,' she breathed.

'Is it really hell?' he murmured.

'No, it's…' she brushed her lips over his '…heaven, if you must know.'

'That's what I thought. Are you trying to warm your hands on my chest?'

'Trying. I don't think I'm having very much luck. You do many things very well, but acting as a human hot-water bottle isn't one of them.'

'No. You could be right. My skills definitely lie in other directions. Perhaps I could demonstrate some of them to you right now.' He moved his hand from her bottom and curled his fingers round hers as he guided her hand towards his groin. 'In which case I think you'd better join me in the shower, don't you?'

She couldn't have said no even if she'd wanted to. One touch from Renzo was like lighting the touch-paper. Two seconds in his arms and she went up in flames.

In the bathroom, he unzipped her drab beige uniform, soft words of Italian falling from his lips as her breasts were revealed to him. Disproportionately big breasts which had always been the bane of her life, because she'd spent her life with men's attention being constantly homed in on them. She'd often thought longingly of a breast reduction—except who could afford an operation like that on the money she earned waiting tables? So she'd made do with wearing restrictive bras, until Renzo had taught her to love her body and told her that her breasts were the most magnificent thing he'd ever seen. To enjoy being suckled or having his teeth tease the sensitive flesh until she was crying out with pleasure. He'd started to buy lingerie for her, too—the only thing she'd ever allowed him to buy for her and only because he'd insisted. He couldn't understand why she wouldn't let him spend money on her, but her reasons were raw and painful and she had no intention of letting him in on her secret.

But she let him buy her pretty underclothes, because he insisted that it enhanced their sex play—balcony bras and tiny matching panties, which he said made the most of her curvy hips. And didn't it make her feel rather decadent when she was at work, knowing she was wearing the finest silk and lace beneath the drab check of her waitress uniform? Hadn't he told her that he *wanted* her to think about him when he wasn't there? That when he was far away on business he liked to imagine her touching herself until she was wet between the legs and her body bucking helplessly as she thought about *him*. And although his fantasy about how she lived when he wasn't there was just that—fantasy—she couldn't deny that it also turned her on. But then, everything about Renzo Sabatini turned her on. His tall and powerful frame. His black hair and black eyes and those dark-rimmed spectacles he wore when he was working on one of his detailed plans. That way he had of watching her as she moved around the room. And stroking her until she was trembling with helpless need for him. Like now.

Her dress fell to the floor and the delicate underwear quickly followed. A master in the art of undressing, her Italian lover was soon as naked as she, and Darcy sucked in an instinctive gasp when she saw how aroused he was.

'Daunting, isn't it?' His sensual lips curved into a mocking smile. 'Want to touch me?'

'Not until I've got hot water gushing over me. My hands are so cold you might recoil.'

'I don't think so,' he said softly.

His eyes glittered as he picked her up and carried her into the wet room, where steaming water streamed down from a huge showerhead and the sensory impact of the experience threatened to overwhelm her. Hot water on icy skin and a naked Renzo in her arms. In the steamy environment, which made her think of a tropical forest, his lips were hungry, one hand stroking between her legs while the other played with one aching nipple. The warm water relaxed her, made her aware of the fierce pounding of her heart and the sudden rush of warmth at her groin. She ran her hands over the hard planes of his body, enjoying the sensation of honed muscle beneath his silken olive skin. Boldly she reached down to circle his erection, sliding her thumb and forefinger lightly up and down the rocky shaft the way she knew he liked it. He gave a groan. Hell. *She* liked it, too. She liked everything he did to her…and the longer it went on, the more difficult it was to imagine a life without him.

She closed her eyes as his fingers moved down over her belly until they were tangling in the wet hair at the juncture of her thighs. One finger took a purposeful route farther, until it was deep inside her and she gave a little yelp of pleasure as he strummed the finger against swollen flesh, the rhythmical movement taking her closer to the edge. And now it was her turn to writhe her hips against him, wanting release—and wanting oblivion, too.

'Now,' she breathed. 'Make love to me now.'

'You are impatient, little one.'

Of course she was impatient. It had been nearly a month since she'd seen him. A month when he'd been hard at work in Japan, before flying to South America to oversee the enormous new hotel complex he'd designed which was creating a lot of waves in the high-octane world of architecture. And yes, there had been the occasional email—an amusing description about a woman who had propositioned him after a boardroom meeting, which Darcy had managed to laugh off and act as if it didn't hurt. He'd even phoned her once, when his plane had been delayed at the airport in Rio de Janeiro and presumably he must have had time to kill. And even though she'd been battling through the wind on her way back from the discount supermarket at the time, she'd managed to find shelter in a shop doorway and make like it was a normal conversation. She'd tried to tell herself that she didn't mind his total lack of commitment. That they didn't have an ordinary relationship and that was what made it so interesting.

He'd told her right from the start what she could expect and what she must not expect, and number one on his list had been commitment, closely followed by love. She remembered turning round as he'd spoken, surprising an unexpectedly bleak look in his gaze—unexpected because those ebony eyes usually gave nothing away. But she hadn't probed further because she'd sensed he would clam up. Actually, she never probed—because if you asked someone too many questions about themselves, they might just turn around and ask them back and that was the last thing she wanted.

And she had agreed to his emotionally cold terms, hadn't she? She'd acted as if they were the most reasonable requests in the world. To be honest, she hadn't been able to think beyond the next kiss—and every kiss had the effect of binding her ever tighter to him. But several months had passed since he'd extracted that agreement from her and time changed everything. It always did. Time made your feelings start to deepen and made you prone to foolish daydreams. And what could be more foolish than imagining some kind of future with the billionaire designer with his jet-set lifestyle and homes all around the world? She, without a single qualification to her name, whose only skill was her ability to multitask in a restaurant?

She pressed her lips against his shoulder, thinking how best to respond to his question—to show him she still had some control left, even if it was slipping away by the second. 'Impatient?' she murmured into his wet, bare skin. 'If I'm going too fast for you, we could always put this on hold and do it later. Have that cup of tea after all. Is that what you'd like, Renzo?'

His answer was swift and unequivocal. Imprisoning her hands, he pushed her up against the granite wall of the wet room, parted her legs and thrust into her, as hot and hard as she'd ever felt him. She gasped as he filled her. She cried out as he began to move. From knowing nothing, he'd taught her everything and she had been his willing pupil. In his arms, she came to life.

'Renzo,' she gasped as he rocked against her.

'Did you miss me, *cara*?'

She closed her eyes. 'I missed…this.'

'But nothing else?'

She wanted to say that there *was* nothing else, but why spoil a beautiful moment? No man would want to hear something like that, would they—even if it was true? Especially not a man with an ego the size of Renzo's. 'Of course,' she said as he stilled inside her. 'I missed you.'

Did he sense that her answer was less than the 100 per cent he demanded of everything and everyone? Was that why he slowed the pace down, dragging her back from the brink of her orgasm to tantalise her with nearly there thrusts until she could bear it no more?

'Renzo—'

'What is it?'

How could he sound so calm? So totally in control. But control was what he was good at, wasn't it? He was the master of control. She squirmed. 'Don't play with me.'

'But I thought you liked me playing with you. Perhaps…' he bent his head to whisper in her water-soaked ear '…I shall make you beg.'

'Oh, no, you won't!' Fiercely, she cupped his buttocks and held him against her and he gave an exultant laugh as at last he gave her exactly what she wanted. He worked on her hard and fast, his deep rhythm taking her up and up, until her shuddered cries were blotted out by his kiss and he made that low groaning sound as he came. It was, she thought, about the only time she'd ever heard him sound helpless.

Afterwards he held her until the trembling had subsided and then soaped her body and washed her hair with hands which were almost gentle—as if he was attempting to make up for the almost-brutal way he'd brought her gasping to orgasm. He dried her carefully, then carried her into the bedroom and placed her down on the vast bed which overlooked the whispering treetops of Eaton Square. The crisp, clean linen felt like heaven against her scented skin as he got into bed beside her and slid his arms around her waist. She was sleepy and suspected he was, too, but surely they needed to have some sort of *conversation* instead of just mating like two animals and then tumbling into oblivion.

But wasn't that all they were, when it boiled down to it? This affair was all about sex. Nothing except sex.

'So how was your time away?' she forced herself to ask.

'You don't want to know.'

'Yes, I do.'

'All good.' He yawned. 'The hotel is almost complete and I've been commissioned to design a new art gallery just outside Tokyo.'

'But you're tired?' she observed.

His voice was mocking. '*Sì, cara.* I'm tired.'

She wriggled her back against him. 'Ever thought of easing off for a while? Taking a back seat and just enjoying your success?'

'Not really.' He yawned again.

'Why not?' she said, some rogue inside her making her persist, even though she could sense his growing impatience with her questions.

His voice grew hard. 'Because men in my position don't *ease off.* There are a hundred hot new architects who would love to be where I am. Take your eye off the ball and you're toast.' He stroked her nipple. 'Why don't you tell me about your week instead?'

'Oh, mine was nothing to speak about. I just *serve* the toast,' she said lightly.

She closed her eyes because she thought that they might sleep but she was wrong because Renzo was cupping her breasts, rubbing his growing erection up against her bottom until she gave an urgent sound of assent and he entered her from behind, where she was slick and ready.

His lips were in her hair and his hands were playing with her nipples as he moved inside her again. Her shuddered capitulation was swift and two orgasms in less than an hour meant she could no longer fight off her fatigue. She fell into a deep sleep and sometime later she felt the bed dip as Renzo got up and when she dragged her eyelids open it was to see that the spring evening was still light. The leaves in the treetops outside the window were golden-green in the fading sunlight and she could hear a distant bird singing.

It felt surreal lying here. The prestigious square on which he lived sometimes seemed like a mirage. All the lush greenery gave the impression of being in the middle of the country—something made possible only by the fact that this was the most expensive real estate in London. But beyond the treetops near his exclusive home lay the London which was *her* city. Discount stores and tower blocks and garbage fluttering on the pavements. Snarled roads and angry drivers. And somewhere not a million miles from here, but which felt as if it might as well be in a different universe, was the tiny bedsit she called home. Sometimes it seemed like something out of some corny old novel—the billionaire boss and his waitress lover. Because things like this didn't usually happen to girls like her.

But Renzo hadn't taken advantage of her, had he? He'd never demanded anything she hadn't wanted to give. She'd accepted his ride home—even though some part of her had cried out that it was unwise. Yet for once in her life she'd quashed the voice of common sense which was as much a part of her as her bright red hair. For years she had simply kept her head down and toed the line in order to survive. But not this time. Instead of doing what she knew she *should* do, she'd succumbed to something she'd really wanted and that something was Renzo. Because she'd never wanted anyone the way she'd wanted him.

What she was certain he'd intended to be just one night had become another and then another as their unconventional relationship had developed. It was a relationship which existed only within the walls of his apartment because, as if by some unspoken agreement, they never went out on dates. Renzo's friends were wealthy and well connected, just like him. Fast-living powerbrokers with influential jobs and nothing in common with someone like her. And anyway, it would be bizarre if they started appearing together in public because they weren't really a *couple*, were they?

She knew their relationship could most accurately be described as 'friends with benefits,' though the benefits heavily outweighed the friendship side and the arrogant Italian had once told her that he didn't really have any female *friends*. Women were for the bedroom and kitchen—he'd actually said that, when he'd been feeling especially uninhibited after one of their marathon sex sessions, which had ended up in the bath. He'd claimed afterwards that he'd been joking but Darcy had recognised a grain of truth behind his words. Even worse was the way his masterful arrogance had thrilled her, even though she'd done her best to wear a disapproving expression.

Because when it boiled down to it, Darcy knew the score. She was sensible enough to know that Renzo Sabatini was like an ice cream cone you ate on a sunny day. It tasted amazing—possibly the most amazing thing you'd ever tasted—but you certainly didn't expect it to last.

She glanced up as he walked back into the bedroom carrying a tray, a task she performed many times a day—the only difference being that he was completely naked.

'You're spoiling me,' she said.

'I'm just returning the favour. I'd like to ask where you learned that delicious method of licking your tongue over my thighs but I realise that—'

'I learned it from you?'

'*Esattamente.*' His eyes glittered. 'Hungry?'

'Thirsty.'

'I expect you are,' he said, bending over to brush his lips over hers.

She took the tea he gave her and watched as he tugged on a pair of jeans and took his glass of red wine over to his desk, sitting down and putting on dark-framed spectacles before waking his computer from sleep mode and beginning to scroll down. After a couple of minutes he was completely engrossed in something on the screen and suddenly Darcy felt completely excluded. With his back on her, she felt like an insignificant cog in the giant wheel which was his life. They'd just had sex—twice—and now he was burying himself in work, presumably until his body had recovered enough to do it to her all over again. And she would just lie back and let him, or climb on top of him if the mood took her—because that was her role. Up until now it had always been enough but suddenly it didn't seem like nearly enough.

Did she signal her irritation? Was that why he rattled out a question spoken like someone who was expecting an apologetic denial as an answer?

'Is something wrong?'

This was her cue to say no, nothing was wrong. To pat the edge of the bed and slant him a compliant smile because that was what she would normally have done. But Darcy wasn't in a compliant mood today. She'd heard a song on the radio just before leaving work. A song which had taken her back to a place she hadn't wanted to go to and the mother she'd spent her life trying to forget.

Yet it was funny how a few random chords could pluck at your heartstrings and make you want to screw up your face and cry. Funny how you could still love someone even though they'd let you down, time after time. That had been the real reason she'd sent Renzo's driver away. She'd wanted to walk to the Tube so that her unexpected tears could mingle with the rain. She'd hoped that by coming here and having her Italian lover take her to bed, it might wipe away her unsettled feelings. But it seemed to have done the opposite. It had awoken a new restlessness in her. It had made her realise that great sex and champagne in the shadows of a powerful man's life weren't the recipe for a happy life—and the longer she allowed it to continue, the harder it would be for her to return to the real world. Her world.

She finished her tea and put the cup down, the subtle taste of peppermint and rose petals still lingering on her lips. It was time for the affair to fade out, like the credits at the end of the film. And even though she was going to miss him like crazy, she was the one who needed to start it rolling.

She made her voice sound cool and non-committal. 'I'm thinking I won't be able to see you for a while.'

That had his attention. He turned away from the screen and, putting his glasses down on the desk, he frowned. 'What are you talking about?'

'I have a week's holiday from work and I'm planning to use it to go to Norfolk.'

She could see he was slightly torn now because he wasn't usually interested in what she did when she wasn't with him, even if he sometimes trotted out a polite question because he obviously felt it was expected of him. But he was interested now.

'What are you doing in Norfolk?'

She shrugged her bare shoulders. 'Looking for a place to rent. I'm thinking of moving there.'

'You mean you're leaving *London*?'

'You sound surprised, Renzo. People leave London all the time.'

'I know. But it's…' He frowned, as if such an option was outside his realm of understanding. 'What's in Norfolk?'

She'd been prepared to let him think that she just wanted a change—which was true —and to leave her real reasons unspoken. But his complete lack of comprehension angered her and when she spoke her voice was low and trembling with an anger which was directed as much at herself as at him.

'Because there I've got the chance of renting somewhere that might have a view of something which isn't a brick wall. As well as a job that doesn't just feature commuters who are so rushed they can barely give me the time of day, let alone a *please* or a thank you. The chance of fresh air and a lower cost of living, plus a pace of life which doesn't wear me out just thinking about it.'

He frowned. 'You mean you don't like where you're living?'

'It's perfectly adequate for my *needs*,' she said carefully. 'Or at least, it has been until now.'

'That's a pretty lukewarm endorsement.' He paused and his frown deepened. 'Is that why you've never invited me round?'

'I guess.' She'd actually done it to save his embarrassment—and possibly hers. She'd tried to imagine him in her humble bedsit eating his dinner off a tray or having to squeeze his towering frame into her tiny bathroom or—even worse—lying on her narrow single bed. It was a laughable concept which would have made them both feel awkward and would have emphasised the vast social gulf between them even more. And that was why she never had. 'Would you really have wanted me to?'

Renzo considered her question. Of course he wouldn't, but he was surprised not to have got an invite. You wouldn't need to be a genius to work out that her life was very different from his and perhaps if he'd been confronted by it then his conscience would have forced him to write a cheque, and this time be more forceful in getting her to accept it. He might have told her to buy some new cushions, or a rug or even a new kitchen, if that was what she wanted. That was how these things usually worked. But Darcy was the proudest woman he'd ever encountered and, apart from the sexy lingerie he'd insisted she wear, had stubbornly refused all his offers of gifts. Why, even his heiress lovers hadn't been averse to accepting diamond necklaces or bracelets or those shoes with the bright red soles. He liked buying women expensive presents—it made him feel he wasn't in any way *beholden* to them. It reduced relationships down to what they really were…transactions. And yet his hard-up little waitress hadn't wanted to know.

'No, I wasn't holding out for an invite,' he said slowly. 'But I thought you might have discussed your holiday plans with me before you went ahead and booked them.'

'But you never discuss your plans with me, Renzo. You just do as you please.'

'You're saying you want me to run my schedule past you first?' he questioned incredulously.

'Of course I don't. You've made it clear that's not the way you operate and I've always accepted that. So you can hardly object if I do the same.'

But she was missing the point and Renzo suspected she knew it. *He* was the one who called the shots because that was also how these things worked. He was the powerbroker in this affair and she was smart enough to realise that. Yet he could see something implacable in her green gaze, some new sense of determination which had settled over her, and something else occurred to him. 'You might stay on in Norfolk,' he said slowly.

'I might.'

'In which case, this could be the last time we see one another.'

She shrugged. 'I guess it could.'

'Just like that?'

'What were you expecting? It had to end sometime.'

Renzo's eyes narrowed thoughtfully. Up until a couple of hours ago it wouldn't *really* have bothered him if he'd been told he would never see her again. Oh, he might have experienced a faint pang of regret and he certainly would have missed her in a physical sense, because he found her enthusiastic lovemaking irresistible. In fact, he would go so far as to say that she was the best lover he'd ever had, probably because he had taught her to be perfectly attuned to the needs of *his* body. But nothing was for ever. He knew that. In a month—maybe less—he would have replaced her with someone else. Someone cool and presentable, who would blend more easily into his life than Darcy Denton had ever done.

But she was the one who was doing the withdrawing and Renzo didn't like that. He was a natural predator—proud and fiercely competitive. Perhaps even prouder than Darcy. Women didn't leave *him*... He was the one who did the walking away—and at a time of *his* choosing. And he still wanted her. He had not yet reached the crucial boredom state which would make him direct her calls straight to voicemail or leave a disproportionately long time before replying to texts. Lazily, he flicked through the options available to him.

'What about if you took a holiday with me, instead of going to Norfolk on your own?'

He could tell from the sudden dilatation of her eyes that the suggestion had surprised her. And the hardening of her nipples above the rumpled bedsheet suggested it had excited her. He felt the sudden beat of blood to his groin and realised it had excited him, too.

Her emerald eyes were wary. 'Are you serious?'

'Why not?'

He got up from the chair, perfectly aware of the powerful effect his proximity would have on her as he sat down on the edge of the bed. 'Is that such an abhorrent suggestion—to take my lover on holiday?'

She shrugged. 'It's not the type of thing we usually do. We usually stay in and don't go out.'

'But life would be very dull if only the expected happened. Are you telling me that the idea of a few days away with me doesn't appeal to you?' He splayed his palm possessively over the warm weight of her breast and watched as her swanlike neck constricted in a swallow.

She chewed on her lip. 'Renzo—'

'Mmm...?'

'It's...it's quite difficult to think straight when you're touching my nipple like that.'

'Thinking in the bedroom can be a very overrated pastime,' he drawled, subtly increasing the pressure of his fingers. 'What's to think about? My proposition is perfectly simple. You could come out to Tuscany with me. I need to make a trip there this weekend. We could spend a few days together and you would still have time to go to Norfolk.'

She leaned back against the pillows and her eyes closed as he continued to massage her breast. 'You have a house there, don't you?' she breathed. 'In Tuscany.'

'Not for much longer. That's why I'm going. I'm selling it.' The pressure on her breast increased as his voice hardened. 'And you can keep me company. I have to take an earlier flight via Paris to do some business but you could always fly out separately.' He paused. 'Doesn't the idea tempt you, Darcy?'

His words filtered into her distracted mind as he continued to tease her exquisitely aroused nipple and her lashes fluttered open. His black eyes were as hard as shards of jet but that didn't affect the magic he was creating with the slow movement of his fingers as she tried to concentrate on his question.

Her tongue flicked out to moisten her lips. Of course a few days away with him tempted her— but it wasn't the thought of flying to Tuscany which was making her heart race like a champion stallion.

He tempted her. Would it be so wrong to grab a last session of loving with him—but in a very different environment? Because although his apartment was unimaginably big, it had its limitations. Despite the pool in the basement, the heated roof terrace and huge screening room, she was starting to feel like part of the fixtures and fittings. Couldn't she go out to Italy and, in the anonymous setting of a foreign country, pretend to be his *real* girlfriend for a change? Someone he really cared about—rather than just someone whose panties he wanted to rip off every time he saw her.

'I guess it does tempt me,' she said. 'A little.'

'Not the most enthusiastic response I've ever had,' he commented. 'But I take it that's a yes?'

'It's a yes,' she agreed, relaxing back into the feathery bank of pillows as he turned his attention to her other aching breast.

'Good.' There was a pause and the circular movement of his fingers halted. 'But first you're going to have to let me buy you some new clothes.'

Her eyes snapped open and she froze—automatically pushing his hand away. 'When will you get it into your thick skull that I'm not interested in your money, Renzo?'

'I think I'm getting the general idea,' he said drily. 'And although your independence is admirable, I find it a little misguided. Why not just accept gracefully? I like giving presents and most women like receiving them.'

'It's a very kind thought and thank you all the same,' she said stiffly, 'but I don't want them.'

'This isn't a question of *want*, more a case of *need*

and I'm afraid that this time I'm going to have to insist,' he said smoothly. 'I have a certain…*position* to maintain in Italy and, as the woman accompanying me, you'll naturally be the focus of attention. I'd hate you to feel you were being judged negatively because you don't have the right clothes.'

'Just as you're judging me right now, you mean?' she snapped.

He shook his head, his lips curving into a slow smile and his deep voice dipping. 'You must have realised by now that I prefer you wearing nothing at all, since nothing looks better than your pale and perfect skin. But although it's one of my biggest fantasies, I really don't think we can have you walking around the Tuscan hills stark naked, do you? I'm just looking out for you, Darcy. Buy yourself a few pretty things. Some dresses you can wear in the evenings. It isn't a big deal.'

She opened her mouth to say that it *was* a big deal to her but he had risen to his feet and his shadow was falling over her so that she was bathed in darkness as she lay there. She looked up into lash-shuttered eyes which gleamed like ebony and her heart gave a funny twist as she thought about how much she was going to miss him. How was she going to return to a life which was empty of her powerful Italian lover? 'What are you doing?' she croaked as he began to unzip his jeans.

'Oh, come on. Use your imagination,' he said softly. 'I'm going to persuade you to take my money.'

CHAPTER TWO

RENZO LOOKED AT his watch and gave a click of impatience. Where the hell *was* she? She *knew* he detested lateness, just as she knew he ran his diary like clockwork. In the exclusive lounge at Florence airport he crossed one long leg over the other, aware that the movement had caused the heads of several women instinctively to turn, but he paid them no attention for there was only one woman currently on his mind—and not in a good way.

The flight he had instructed Darcy to catch—in fact, to purchase a first-class ticket for—had discharged its passengers twenty minutes earlier and she had not been among their number. His eyes had narrowed as he'd stared at the hordes of people streaming through the arrivals section, fully expecting to see her eagerly pushing her way through to see him, her pale face alight with excitement and her curvy body resplendent in fine new clothes—but there had been no sight of her. A member of staff had dealt with his irritation and was currently checking the flight list while he was forced to consider the unbelievable... *that she might have changed her mind about joining him in Italy.*

He frowned. Had her reluctance to take the cash he had insisted she accept gone deeper than he'd imagined? He'd thought she was simply making a gesture—hiding the natural greed which ran through the veins of pretty much every woman—but perhaps he had misjudged her. Perhaps she really *was* deeply offended by his suggestion that she buy herself some decent clothes.

Or maybe she'd just taken the money and done a runner, not intending to come here and meet him at all.

Renzo's mouth hardened, because wasn't there a rogue thought flickering inside his head which almost wished that to be the case? Wouldn't he have welcomed a sound reason to despise her, instead of this simmering resentment that she was preparing to take her leave of him? That she had been the one to make a decision which was usually *his* province. He glanced again at his wristwatch. And how ironic that the woman to call time on a relationship should be a busty little red-headed waitress he'd picked up in a cocktail bar rather than one of the many more eligible women he'd dated.

He hadn't even been intending to go out the night he'd met her. He'd just planned to have a quick drink with a group of bankers he'd known from way back who had been visiting from Argentina and wanted to see some London nightlife. Renzo didn't particularly like nightclubs and remembered the stir the six men had made as they'd walked into the crowded Starlight Room at the Granchester Hotel, where they'd ordered champagne and decided which of the women sipping cocktails they should ask to dance. But Renzo hadn't been interested in the svelte women who had been smiling invitingly in his direction. His attention had been caught by the curviest little firecracker he'd ever seen. She'd looked as if she had been poured into the black satin dress which had skimmed her rounded hips, but it had been her breasts which had caused the breath to dry in his throat. *Madonna, che bella!* What breasts! Luscious and quivering, they had a deep cleavage he wanted to run his tongue over and that first sight of them was something he would remember for as long as he lived.

He had ended up dancing with no one, mainly because he'd been too busy watching her and his erection had been too painful for him to move without embarrassment. He'd ordered drinks only from her, and wondered afterwards if she noticed he left them all. Each time he'd summoned her over to his table he could sense the almost palpable electricity which sizzled in the air—he'd certainly never felt such a powerful attraction towards a total stranger before. He'd expected her to make some acknowledgement of the silent chemistry which pulsed between them, but she hadn't. In fact the way her eyelids had half shielded her huge green eyes and the cautious looks she'd been directing at him had made him think she must either be the world's greatest innocent, or its most consummate actress. If he had known it was the former, would he still have pursued her?

Of course he would. Deep down he recognised he wouldn't have been able to stop himself because hadn't he been gripped by a powerful hunger which insisted he would never know peace until he had possessed her?

He'd been waiting outside when eventually she had emerged from the club and had thanked the heavens for the heavy downpour of rain which had been showering down on her. She hadn't looked a bit surprised to see him as she'd opened up her umbrella and for a moment it had crossed his mind that she might take a different man home with her every night, though even that had not been enough to make him order his driver to move on. But when he'd offered her a lift she'd refused, in an emphatic manner which had startled him.

'No, thanks.'

'No?'

'I know what you want,' she'd said, in a low voice. 'And you won't get it from me.'

And with that she'd disappeared into the rain-wet night and Renzo had sat in the back seat of the limousine, watching her retreating form beneath her little black umbrella, his mouth open and his body aching with frustration and unwilling admiration.

He'd gone to the club the next night and the weekend when he'd returned from a work trip to New York. Some nights she'd been there and some she hadn't. He'd discovered she only worked there at weekends and it had only been later he'd found out she had a daytime job as a waitress somewhere else. Extracting information from her had been like trying to get blood from a stone. She was the most private woman he'd ever met as well as the most resistant and perhaps it was those things which made Renzo persist in a way he'd never had to persist before. And just when he'd been wondering if he was wasting his time, she had agreed to let him drive her home.

His voice had been wry as he'd looked at her. *'Madonna mia!* You mean you've decided you trust me enough to accept the lift?'

Her narrow shoulders had shrugged, causing her large breasts to jiggle beneath the shiny black satin of her dress and sending a shaft of lust arrowing straight to his groin. 'I guess so. All the other staff have seen you by now and you've been captured on CCTV for all eternity, so if you're a murderer then you'll be apprehended soon enough.'

'Do I look like a murderer?'

She had smiled then, and it had been like the sun coming out from behind a cloud.

'No. Although you look just a little bit dangerous.'

'Women always tell me that's a plus.'

'I'm sure they do, though I'm not sure I agree. Anyway, it's a filthy night, so I might as well get a lift with you. But I haven't changed my mind,' she'd added fiercely. 'And if you think I'm going to sleep with you, then you're wrong.'

As it happened, she was the one who'd been wrong. They'd driven through the dark wet streets of London and he'd asked her to come in for coffee, not thinking for a moment she'd accept. But maybe the chemistry had been just as powerful for her. Maybe her throat had also been tight with tension and longing and she'd been finding it as difficult to speak as he had, as she'd sat beside him in the leather-scented car. He'd driven her to his apartment and she'd told him primly that she didn't really like coffee. So he'd made her tea flavoured with peppermint and rose petals, and for the first time in his life he'd realised he might lose her if he rushed it. He'd wondered afterwards if it was his unfamiliar restraint which had made her relax and sink into one of his huge sofas—so that when at last he'd leaned over to kiss her she'd been all quivering acquiescence. He'd done it to her right there—pulling her panties down and plunging right into her—terrified she might change her mind during the long walk from the sitting room to the bedroom.

And that had been when he'd discovered she was a virgin—and in that moment something had changed. The world had tipped on its axis because he'd never had sex with a virgin before and had been unprepared for the rush of primitive satisfaction which had flooded through him. As they'd lain there afterwards, gasping for breath among all the cushions, he'd pushed a damp curl away from her dewy cheek, demanding to know why she hadn't told him.

'Why would I? Would you have stopped?'

'No, but I could have laid you at the centre of my big bed instead of the sofa if I'd known this was your first sexual adventure.'

'What, you mean like some sort of medieval sacrifice?' she'd murmured and that had confused him, too, because he would have expected high emotion at such a moment, not such a cool response.

Had it been her coolness which had made him desire her even more? Possibly. He'd thought it would be one night, but he'd been mistaken. He'd never dated a waitress before and he acknowledged the cold streak of snobbery in his nature which told him it would be unwise to buck that trend. But Darcy had confounded him. She read just as many books as an academic he'd once dated—although admittedly, she preferred novels to molecular biology. And she didn't follow the predictable path of most women in a sexual relationship. She didn't bore him with stories of her past, nor weigh him down with questions about his own. Their infrequent yet highly satisfying meetings, which involved a series of mind-blowing orgasms, seemed to meet both their needs. She seemed instinctively to understand that he wasn't seeking a close or lasting connection with a woman. Not now and not ever.

But sometimes an uncomfortable question strayed into his mind to ask why such a beauty would have so willingly submitted her virginity to a total stranger. And didn't he keep coming up with the troublesome answer that maybe she had been holding out for the highest bidder—in this case, an Italian billionaire...?

'Renzo?'

The sound of her voice dragged him away back into the present and Renzo looked up to see a woman walking through the airport lounge towards him, pulling behind her a battered suitcase on wheels. His eyes narrowed. It was Darcy, yes—but not Darcy as he knew her, in her drab waitress uniform or pale and naked against his pristine white sheets. Renzo blinked. This was Darcy in a dress the colour of sunshine, dotted with tiny blue flowers. It was a simple cotton dress but the way she wore it was remarkable. It wasn't the cut or the label which was making every man in the place stare at her—it was her youthful body and natural beauty. Fresh and glowing, her bare arms and legs were honed by honest hard work rather than mindless sessions in the gym. She looked *radiant* and the natural bounce of her breasts meant that no man could look at her without thinking about procreation. Renzo's mouth dried. Procreation had never been on *his* agenda, but sex most definitely was. He wanted to pull her hungrily into his arms and to kiss her hard on the mouth and feel those soft breasts crushing against him. But Renzo Sabatini would never be seen in any airport—let alone one in his homeland—making such a public demonstration of affection.

And wasn't it time he reinforced the fact that nobody—nobody—ever kept him waiting?

'You're late,' he said repressively, throwing aside his newspaper and rising to his feet.

Darcy nodded. She could sense his irritation but that didn't affect her enjoyment of the way he was looking at her—if only to reassure her she hadn't made a terrible mistake in choosing a cheap cotton dress instead of the clothes he must have been expecting her to wear. Still, since this was going to be the holiday of a lifetime it was important she got it off to a good start and the truth of it was that she *was* late. In fact, she'd started to worry if she would get here at all because that horrible vomiting bug she'd had at the beginning of the week had really laid her low.

'Yes, I know. I'm sorry about that.'

He commandeered her wheeled case and winced slightly as he took her hand luggage. 'What have you got in here? Bricks?'

'I put in a few books,' she said as they set off towards the exit. 'Though I wasn't sure how much time I'd have for reading.'

Usually he would have made a provocative comment in response to such a remark but he didn't and the unyielding expression on his face told her he wasn't ready to forgive her for making him wait. But he didn't say anything as they emerged into the bright sunshine and Darcy was too overcome by the bluest sky she'd ever seen to care.

'Oh, Renzo—I can't believe I'm in Italy. It's so beautiful,' she enthused as she looked around, but still he didn't answer. In fact, he didn't speak until his shiny black car had pulled out of the airport and was heading towards a signpost marked Chiusi.

'I've been waiting at the damned airport for over an hour,' he snapped. 'Why weren't you on the flight I told you to get?'

Darcy hesitated. She supposed she could come up with some vague story to placate him but hadn't she already shrouded so much of her life with evasion and secrets, terrified that someone would examine it in the harsh light of day and judge her? Why add yet another to the long list of things she needed to conceal? And this was different. This wasn't something she was ashamed of—so why not be upfront about the decision she'd made when he had stuffed that enormous wad of cash into her hand and made her feel deeply uncomfortable?

'Because it was too expensive.'

'Darcy, I *gave* you the money to get that flight.'

'I know you did and it was very generous of you.' She drew in a deep breath. 'But when I saw how much it cost to fly to Florence first class, I just couldn't do it.'

'What do you mean, you couldn't do it?'

'It seemed a ludicrous amount of money to spend on a two-hour flight so I bought a seat on a budget airline instead.'

'You did *what*?'

'You should try it sometime. It's true they ran out of sandwiches and the tea was stone-cold, but I saved absolutely loads of money because the price difference was massive. Just like I did with the clothes.'

'The clothes,' he repeated uncomprehendingly.

'Yes. I went to that department store you recommended on Bond Street but the clothes were stupidly overpriced. I couldn't believe how much they were asking for a simple T-shirt so I went to the high street and found some cheaper versions, like this dress.' She smoothed the crisp yellow cotton down over her thighs and her voice wavered a little uncertainly. 'Which I think looks okay, doesn't it?'

He flashed a glance to where her hand was resting. 'Sure,' he said, his voice sounding thick. 'It looks okay.'

'So what's the problem?'

He slammed the palm of his hand against the steering wheel. 'The problem is that I don't like being disobeyed.'

She laughed. 'Oh, Renzo. You sound like a headmaster. You're not my teacher, you know—and I'm not your pupil.'

'Oh, really?' He raised his eyebrows. 'I thought I'd been responsible for teaching you rather a lot.'

His words made her face grow hot as they zoomed past blue-green mountains, but suddenly Darcy was finding the sight of Renzo's profile far more appealing than the Tuscan countryside. He was so unbelievably gorgeous. Just the most gorgeous man she'd ever seen. Would she ever feel this way about anyone again, she wondered—with a chest which became so tight when she looked at him that sometimes it felt as if she could hardly *breathe*? Probably not. It had never happened before, so what were the chances of it happening again? How had Renzo himself described what had happened when they first met? *Colpo di fulmine*—that was it. A lightning strike—which everyone knew was extremely rare. It was about the only bit of Italian she knew.

She sneaked another glance at him. His black hair was ruffled and his shirt was open at the neck—olive skin glowing gold and stunningly illuminated by the rich Tuscan light. His thighs looked taut beneath his charcoal trousers and Darcy could feel the sudden increase of her pulse as her gaze travelled along their muscular length. She'd rarely been in a car with him since the night he had seduced her—or rather, when she had fallen greedily into his arms. She'd hardly been *anywhere* with him other than the bedroom and suddenly she was glad about something which might have bothered other women.

Because with the amazing landscape sliding past like a TV commercial, she thought how easy it would be to get used to this kind of treatment. Not just the obvious luxury of being driven through such beautiful countryside, but the chance to be a bona fide couple like this. And she mustn't get used to it, because it was a one-off. One last sweet taste of Renzo Sabatini before she began her new life in Norfolk and started to forget him—the man with the cold heart who had taught her the definition of pleasure. The precise and brilliant architect who turned into a tiger in the bedroom.

'So what exactly are we going to be doing when we get to this place of yours?' she said.

'You mean apart from making love?'

'Apart from that,' she agreed, almost wishing he hadn't said it despite the instant spring of her breasts in response. Did he need to keep drumming in her sole purpose in his life? She remembered the hiking shoes she'd packed and wondered if she'd completely misjudged the situation. Was he planning to show her anything of Tuscany, or would they simply be doing the bed thing, only in a more glamorous location? She wondered if he had sensed her sudden discomfiture and if that was the reason for his swift glance as they left the motorway for a quieter road.

'The man who is buying the estate is coming for dinner,' he said, by way of explanation.

'Oh? Is that usual?'

'Not really, but he's actually my lawyer and I want to persuade him to keep on the staff who have worked at Vallombrosa for so long. He's bringing his girl-friend with him, so it'll be good to have you there to balance the numbers.'

Darcy nodded. To balance the numbers. Of course. She was there to fill an empty chair and warm the ty-coon's bed—there was nothing more to it than that. Stupidly, his remark hurt but she didn't show it—something in which she'd learned to excel. A child-hood of deprivation and fear had taught her to hide her feelings behind a mask and present the best ver-sion of herself to the world. The version that prospec-tive foster parents might like if they were looking for a child to fit into their lovely home. And if sometimes she wondered what she might reveal if that mask ever slipped, she didn't worry about it for too long because she was never going to let that happen.

'So when were you last abroad?' he questioned, as they passed a pretty little hilltop village.

'Oh, not for ages,' she answered vaguely.

'How come?'

It was a long time since she'd thought about it and Darcy stared straight ahead as she remembered the charity coach trip to Spain when she'd been fifteen. When the blazing summer sun had burned her fair skin and the mobile home on the campsite had felt like sleeping in a hot tin can. They were supposed to be grateful that the church near the children's home had raised enough money to send them on the supposed trip of a lifetime and she had really tried to be grateful. Until somebody had drilled a peephole into the wall of the female showers and there had been a huge fuss about it. And someone had definitely stolen two pairs of her knickers when she'd been out swimming in the overcrowded pool. Somehow she didn't think Renzo Sabatini's Tuscan villa was going to be anything like that. 'I went on a school trip when I was a teenager,' she said. 'That was the only time I've been abroad.'

He frowned. 'You're not much of a traveller, then?'

'You could say that.'

And suddenly Darcy scented danger. On the journey over she'd been worried she might do something stupid. Not something obvious, like using the wrong knife and fork at a fancy dinner, because her waitressing career had taught her everything there was to know about cutlery.

But she realised she'd completely overlooked the fact that proximity might make her careless. Might make her tongue slip and give something away—

something which would naturally repulse him. Renzo had told her that one of the things he liked about her was that she didn't besiege him with questions, or try to *dig deep* to try to understand him better. But that had been a two-way street and the fact he didn't ask about *her* past had suited her just fine. More than fine. She didn't want to tell any lies but she knew she could never tell him the truth. Because there was no point. There was no future in this liaison of theirs, so why tell him about the junkie mother who had given birth to her? Why endure the pain of seeing his lips curve with shock and contempt as had happened so often in the past? In a world where everyone was striving for perfection and judging you, it hadn't taken her long to realise that the best way to get on in life was to bury all the darkness just as deep as she could.

But thoughts of her mother stabbed at her conscience, prompting her to address something which had been bothering her on the flight over.

'You know the money I saved on my airfare and clothes?' she began.

'Yes, Darcy. I know. You were making a point.' He shot her a glance, his lips curving into a sardonic smile. 'Rich man with too much money shown by poor girl just how much he could save if he bothered to shop around. I get the picture.'

'There's no need to be sarcastic, Renzo,' she said stiffly. 'I want you to have it back. I've put most of it in an envelope in my handbag.'

'But I don't want it back. When are you going to get the message? I have more than enough money. And if it makes you feel better, I admire your resourcefulness and refusal to be seduced by my wealth. It's rare.'

For a moment there was silence. 'I think we both know it wasn't your wealth which seduced me, Renzo.'

She hadn't meant to say it but her quiet words reverberated around the car in an honest explanation of what had first drawn her to him. Not his money, nor his power—but him. The most charismatic and compelling man she'd ever met. She heard him suck in an unsteady breath.

'Madonna mia,' he said softly. 'Are you trying to tempt me into taking the next turning and finding the nearest layby so that I can do what I have been longing to do to you since last I saw you?'

'Renzo—'

'I don't want the damned money you saved! I want you to put your hand in my lap and feel how hard I am for you.'

'Not while you're driving,' said Darcy and although she was disappointed he had turned the emotional into the sexual, she didn't show it. Because that was the kind of man he was, she reminded herself. He was never emotional and always sexual. She didn't need to touch him to know he was aroused—a quick glance and she could see for herself the hard ridge outlined beneath the dark trousers. Suddenly her lips grew dry in response and she licked them, wishing they *could* have sex right then. Because sex stopped you longing for things you were never going to have. Things other women took for granted—like a man promising to love and protect you. Things which seemed as distant as those faraway mountains. With an effort she dragged her attention back to the present. 'Tell me about this place we're going to instead.'

'You think talking about property is a suitable substitute for discovering what you're wearing underneath that pretty little dress?'

'I think it's absolutely vital if you intend keeping your mind on the road, which is probably the most sensible option if you happen to be driving a car.'

'Oh, Darcy.' He gave a soft laugh. 'Did I ever tell you that one of the things I admire about you is your ability to always come up with a smart answer?'

'The *house*, Renzo. I want to talk about the house.'

'Okay. The house. It's old,' he said as he overtook a lorry laden with a towering pile of watermelons. 'And it stands against a backdrop that Leonardo should have painted, instead of that village south of Piacenza which is not nearly as beautiful. It has orchards and vineyards and olive groves—in fact, we produce superb wines from the Sangiovese grape and enough olive oil to sell to some of the more upmarket stores in London and Paris.'

The few facts he'd recited could have been lifted straight from the pages of an estate agent's website and Darcy felt oddly disappointed. 'It sounds gorgeous,' she said dutifully.

'It is.'

'So…why are you selling it?'

He shrugged. 'It's time.'

'Because?'

Too late, she realised she had asked one question too many. His face grew dark, as if the sun had just dipped behind a cloud and his shadowed jaw set itself into a hard and obdurate line.

'Isn't one of the reasons for our unique chemistry that you don't plague me with questions?'

She heard the sudden darkness underpinning his question. 'I was only—'

'Well, don't. Don't pry. Why change what up until now has been a winning formula?' His voice had harshened as he cut through her words, his hands tensing as a discreet sign appeared among the tangle of greenery which feathered the roadside. 'And anyway. We're here. This is Vallombrosa.'

But his face was still dark as the car began to ascend a tree-lined track towards an imposing pair of dark wrought-iron gates which looked like the gates of heaven.

Or the gates of hell, Darcy thought with a sudden flash of foreboding.

CHAPTER THREE

'How on earth am I going to converse with every-one?' questioned Darcy as she stepped out onto the sunny courtyard. 'Since my Italian is limited to the few words I learnt from the phrasebook on the plane and that phrase about the lightning strike?'

'All my staff are bilingual,' Renzo said, his show of bad temper in the car now seemingly forgotten. 'And perfectly comfortable with speaking your mother tongue.'

The words mocked her and Darcy chewed on her lip as she looked away. Mother tongue? Her own mother had taught her to say very little—other than things which could probably have had her prosecuted if she'd repeated them to the authorities.

'Pass Mummy that needle, darling.'

'Pass Mummy those matches.'

'If the policewoman asks if you've met that man before, tell her no.'

But she smiled brightly as she entered the shaded villa and shook hands with Gisella, the elderly house-keeper, and her weather-beaten husband, Pasquale, who was one of the estate's gardeners. A lovely young woman with dark hair helped Gisella around the house and Darcy saw her blush when Renzo introduced her as Stefania. There was also a chef called Donato, who apparently flew in from Rome whenever Renzo was in residence. Donato was tanned, athletic, amazingly good-looking and almost certainly gay.

'Lunch will be in an hour,' he told them. 'But sooner if you're hungry?'

'Oh, I think we can wait,' said Renzo. He turned to Darcy. 'Why don't we take a quick look around while our bags are taken to our room?'

Darcy nodded, thinking how *weird* it felt to be deferred to like that—and to be introduced to his staff just like a real girlfriend. But then she reminded herself that this was only going to work if she didn't allow herself to get carried away. She followed him outside, blinking a little as she took in the vastness of his estate and, although she was seeing only a fraction of it, her senses were instantly overloaded by the beauty of Vallombrosa. Honeybees flitted over purple spears of lavender, vying for space with brightly coloured butterflies. Little lizards basked on baked grey stone. The high walls surrounding the ancient house were covered with scrambling pink roses and stone arches framed the blue-green layers of the distant mountains beyond. Darcy wondered what it must be like growing up somewhere like here, instead of the greyness of the institution in the north of England, which had been the only place she'd ever really called home.

'Like it?' he questioned.

'How could I not? It's beautiful.'

'You know, you're pretty beautiful yourself,' he said softly as he turned his head to look at her.

Remembering the way he'd snapped at her in the car, she wanted to resist him, but the light touch of his hand on her hip and brush of his fingers against her thighs made resistance impossible and Darcy was shaking with longing by the time they reached the shuttered dimness of his bedroom. It was a vast wood-beamed room but there was no time to take in her surroundings because he was pulling her into his arms, his lips brushing hungrily over hers and his fingers tangling themselves in her curls.

'Renzo,' she said unsteadily.

'What?'

She licked her lips. 'You know what.'

'I think I do.' His lips curved into a hard smile. 'You want this?'

Sliding down the zip of her cotton dress, he peeled it away from her and she felt the rush of air against her skin as it pooled to the ground around her ankles. 'Yes,' she breathed. 'That's what I want.'

'Do you know,' he questioned as he unclipped her lacy bra and it joined the discarded dress, 'how much I have been fantasising about you? About this?'

She nodded. 'Me, too,' she said softly, because the newness of the environment and the situation in which she found herself was making her feel almost *shy* in his presence.

But not for long. The beat of her heart and the heat of her blood soon overwhelmed her and had her fumbling for his belt, her fingers trembling with need. Very quickly she was naked and so was he—soft, shuttered light shading their bodies as he pushed her down onto the bed and levered his powerful form over hers. She gripped at the silken musculature of his broad shoulders as he slowly stroked his thumb over her clitoris. And she came right then—so quickly it was almost embarrassing. He laughed softly and eased himself into her wet heat and for a moment he was perfectly still.

'Do you know how good that feels?' he said as he began to move inside her.

She swallowed. 'I've… I've got a pretty good idea.'

'Oh, Darcy. It's you,' he groaned, his eyes closing. 'Only you.'

He said the words like a ragged prayer or maybe a curse—but Darcy didn't read anything into them because she knew exactly what he meant. She was the first and only woman with whom he hadn't needed to wear a condom, because her virginity had elevated her to a different status from his other lovers—he'd told her that himself. He told her she was truly pure. He'd been fascinated to find a woman of twenty-four who'd never had a lover before and by her fervent reply when he'd asked if she ever wanted children.

'Never!'

Her response must have been heartfelt enough to convince him because in a rare moment of confidence he told her he felt exactly the same. Soon afterwards he had casually suggested she might want to go on the pill and Darcy had eagerly agreed. She remembered the first time they'd left the condom off and how it had felt to have his naked skin against hers instead of *'that damned rubber'*—again, his words—between them. It had been…*delicious*. She had felt dangerously close to him and had needed to give herself a stern talking-to afterwards. She'd told herself that the powerful feelings she was experiencing were purely physical. Of course sex felt better without a condom—but it didn't *mean* anything.

But now, in the dimness of his Tuscan bedroom, he was deep inside her. He was filling her and thrusting into her body and kissing her mouth until it throbbed and it felt so amazing that she could have cried. Did her low, moaning sigh break his rhythm? Was that why, with a deft movement, he turned her over so that she was on top of him, his black eyes capturing hers?

'Ride me, *cara*,' he murmured. 'Ride me until you come again.'

She nodded as she tensed her thighs against his narrow hips because she liked this position. It gave her a rare feeling of power, to see Renzo lying underneath her—his eyes half-closed and his lips parted as she rocked back and forth.

She heard his groan and bent her head to kiss it quiet, though she was fairly sure that the walls of this ancient house were deep enough to absorb the age-old sounds of sex. He tangled his hands in her hair, digging his fingers into the wayward curls until pleasure—intense and unalterable—started spiralling up inside her. She came just before he did, gasping as he clasped her hips tightly and hearing him utter something urgent in Italian as his body bucked beneath her. She bent her head to his neck, hot breath panting against his skin until she'd recovered enough to peel herself away from him, before falling back against the mattress.

She looked at the dark beams above her head and the engraved glass lampshade, which looked as if it was as old as the house itself. Someone had put a small vase of scented roses by the window—the same roses

which had been scrambling over the walls outside—
and all the light in that shadowy room seemed to be
centred on those pale pink petals.

'Well,' she said eventually. 'That was some welcome.'

Deliberately, Renzo kept his eyes closed and his
breathing steady because he didn't want to talk.
Not right now. He didn't need to be told how good
it was—that was a given—not when his mind was
busy with the inevitable clamour of his thoughts.

He'd felt a complex mixture of stuff as he'd driven
towards the house, knowing soon it would be under
different ownership. A house which had been in his
mother's family for generations and which had had
more than its fair share of heartbreak. Other people
might have offloaded it years ago but pride had made
him hold on to it, determined to replace bad memories with good ones, and to a large extent he'd succeeded. But you couldn't live in the past. It was time
to let the place go—to say goodbye to the last clinging fragments of yesterday.

He looked across the bed, where Darcy was lying
with her eyes closed, her bright red hair spread all
over the white pillow. He thought about her going to
Norfolk when they got back to London and tried to
imagine what it might be like sleeping with someone
else when she was no longer around, but the idea of
some slender-hipped brunette lying amid his tumbled
sheets was failing to excite him. Instinctively he flattened his palm over her bare thigh.

'And was it the perfect welcome?' he questioned
at last.

'You know it was.' Her voice was sleepy. 'Though

I should go and pick my dress up. It's the first time I've worn it.'

'Don't worry about it.' He smiled. 'I'll have Gisella launder it for you.'

'There's no need for that.' Her voice was suddenly sharp as her eyes snapped open. 'I can do my own washing. I can easily rinse it out in the sink and hang it out to dry in that glorious sunshine.'

'And if I told you I'd rather you didn't?'

'Too bad.'

'Why are you so damned stubborn, Darcy?'

'I thought you *liked* my stubbornness.'

'When appropriate, I do.'

'You mean, when it suits *you*?'

'*Esattamente.*'

She lay back and looked up at the ceiling. How could she explain that she'd felt his housekeeper looking at her and seeing exactly who she was—a servant, just as Gisella was. Like Gisella, she waited tables and cleared up around people who had far more money than she had. That was who she was. She didn't want to look as if she'd suddenly acquired airs and graces by asking to have her clothes laundered. She wasn't going to try to be someone she wasn't—someone who would find it impossible to settle back into her humble world when she got back to England and her billionaire lover was nothing but a distant memory.

But she shouldn't take it out on Renzo, because he was just being Renzo. She'd never objected to his high-handedness before. If the truth were known, she'd always found it a turn-on—and in a way, his arrogance had provided a natural barrier. It had stopped her falling completely under his spell, forcing her to be realistic rather than dreamy. She leaned over and brushed her mouth against his. 'So tell me what you've got planned for us.'

His fingers slid between the tops of her thighs. 'Plans? What plans? The sight of your body seems to have completely short-circuited my brain.'

Halting his hand before it got any further, Darcy enjoyed her brief feeling of power. 'Tell me something about Vallombrosa—and I'm not talking olive or wine production this time. Did you live here when you were a little boy?'

His shuttered features grew wary. 'Why the sudden interest?'

'Because you told me we'd be having dinner with the man who's buying the place. It's going to look a bit odd if I don't know anything about your connection with it. Did you grow up here?'

'No, I grew up in Rome. Vallombrosa was our holiday home.'

'And?' she prompted.

'And it had been in my mother's family for generations. We used it to escape the summer heat of the city. She and I used to come here for the entire vacation and my father would travel down at weekends.'

Darcy nodded because she knew that, like her, he was an only child and that both his parents were dead. And that was pretty much all she knew.

She circled a finger over the hardness of his flat belly. 'So what did you do when you were here?'

He pushed her hand in the direction of his groin. 'My father taught me to hunt and to fish, while my mother socialised and entertained. Sometimes friends came to visit and my mother's school friend Mariella always seemed to be a constant fixture. We were happy, or so I thought.'

Darcy held her breath as something dark and steely entered his voice. 'But you weren't?'

'No. We weren't.' He turned his head to look at her, a hard expression suddenly distorting his features. 'Haven't you realised by now that so few people are?'

'I guess,' she said stiffly. But she'd thought...

What? That other people were strangers to the pain she'd suffered? That someone as successful and as powerful as Renzo had never known emotional deprivation? Was that why he was so distant sometimes—so shuttered and cold? 'Did something happen?'

'You could say that. They got divorced when I was seven.'

'And was it...acrimonious?'

He shot her an unfathomable look. 'Aren't all divorces acrimonious?'

She shrugged. 'I guess.'

'Especially when you discover that your mother's best "friend" has been having an affair with your father for years,' he added, his voice bitter. 'It makes you realise that when the chips are down, women can never be trusted.'

Darcy chewed on her lip. 'So what happened?'

'After the divorce, my father married his mistress but my mother never really recovered. It was a double betrayal and her only weapon was me.'

'Weapon?' she echoed.

He nodded. 'She did everything in her power to keep my father out of my life. She was depressed.' His jaw tightened. 'And believe me, there isn't much a child can do if his mother is depressed. He is—

quite literally—helpless. I used to sit in the corner of the room, quietly making houses out of little plastic bricks while she sobbed her heart out and raged against the world. By the end of that first summer, I'd constructed an entire city.'

She nodded in sudden understanding. Had his need to control been born out of that helplessness? Had the tiny plastic city he'd made been the beginnings of his brilliant architectural career? 'Oh, Renzo—that's... *terrible*,' she said.

He curled his fingers over one breast. 'What an innocent you are, Darcy,' he observed softly.

Darcy felt guilt wash over her. He thought she was a goody-goody because she suspected he was one of those men who divided women into two types— Madonna or whore. Her virginity had guaranteed her Madonna status but it wasn't that simple and if he knew why she had kept herself pure he would be shocked. Married men having affairs was hardly ground-breaking stuff, even if they chose to do it with their wife's best friend—but she could tell him things about *her* life which would make his own story sound like something you could read to a child at bedtime.

And he wasn't asking about *her* past, was he? He wasn't interested—and maybe she ought to be grateful for that. There was no point in dragging out her dark secrets at this late stage in their relationship and ruining their last few days together. 'So what made you decide to sell the estate?'

There was a pause. 'My stepmother died last year,' he said flatly. 'She'd always wanted this house and I suppose I was making sure she never got her hands on it. But now she's gone—they've all gone—and somehow my desire to hang on to it died with her. The estate is too big for a single man to maintain. It needs a family.'

'And you don't want one?'

'I thought we'd already established that,' he said and now his voice had grown cool. 'I saw enough lying and deceit to put me off marriage for a lifetime. Surely you can understand that?'

Darcy nodded. Oh, yes, she understood all right. Just as she recognised that his words were a warning. A warning not to get too close. That just because she was here with him in the unfamiliar role of girlfriend, nothing had really changed. The smile she produced wasn't as bright as usual, but it was good enough to convince him she didn't care. 'Shouldn't we think about getting ready for lunch?' she questioned, her voice growing a little unsteady as his hand moved from her breast to the dip of her belly. 'Didn't…didn't Donato say it would be ready in an hour?'

The touch of her bare skin drove all thoughts from Renzo's mind until he was left with only one kind of hunger. The best kind. The kind which obliterated everything except pleasure. He'd told her more than he usually told anyone and he put that down to the fact that usually she didn't ask. But she needed to know that there would be no more confidences from now on. She needed to know that there was only one reason she was here—and the glint of expectation in her eyes told him that she was getting the message loud and clear. He felt his erection grow exquisitely hard as he looked at the little waitress who somehow knew how to handle him better than any other woman.

'I employ Donato to work to my time frame, not

his,' he said arrogantly, bending his head and sucking at her nipple.

'Oh, Renzo.' Her eyes closed as she fell back against the pillow.

'Renzo, what?' he taunted.

'Don't make me beg.'

He slid his finger over her knee. 'But I like it when you beg.'

'I know you do.'

'So?'

She groaned as her hips lifted hungrily towards his straying finger. 'Please...'

'That's better.' He gave a low and triumphant laugh as he pulled her towards him. 'Lunch can wait,' he added roughly, parting her thighs and positioning himself between them once more. 'I'm afraid this can't.'

CHAPTER FOUR

'THIS?' DARCY HELD up a glimmering black sheath, then immediately waved a flouncy turquoise dress in front of it. 'Or this?'

'The black,' Renzo said, flicking her a swift glance before continuing to button up his shirt.

Her skin now tanned a delicate shade of gold, Darcy slithered into the black dress, aware that Renzo was watching her reflection in the glass in the way a hungry dog might look at a butcher, but she didn't care. She found herself wishing she had the ability to freeze time and that the weekend wasn't drawing to a close because it had been the best few days of her life.

They'd explored his vast estate, scrambling up hilly roads to be rewarded with spectacular views of blue-green mountains and the terracotta smudge of tiny villages. Her hiking boots had come in useful after all! He'd taken her to a beautiful village called Panicale, where they'd drunk coffee in the cobbled square with church bells chiming in stereophonic all around them. And even though Renzo had assured her that May temperatures were too cold for swimming, Darcy wasn't having any of it. She'd never been anywhere with a private pool before—let alone a pool as vast and inviting as the one at Vallombrosa.

Initially a little shy about appearing in her tiny bikini, she'd been quickly reassured by the darkening response in his eyes—though she'd been surprised when he'd changed his mind and decided to join her in the pool after all. And Renzo in sleek black swim shorts, olive skin gleaming as he shook water from his hair, was a vision which made her heart race. She could have spent all afternoon watching his powerful body ploughing through the silky water. But he'd brought her lazy swim to a swift conclusion with some explicit suggestions whispered in her ear and they had returned to his bedroom for sex which had felt even more incredible than usual.

Was it because her senses had been heightened by fresh air and sunshine that everything felt so amazing? Or because Renzo had seemed unusually accessible in this peaceful place which seemed a world away from the hustle and bustle of her normal life? Darcy kept reminding herself that the reasons why were irrelevant. Because this was only temporary. A last trip before she moved to Norfolk—which was probably the only reason he had invited her to join him. And tonight was their final dinner, when they were being joined by Renzo's lawyer, who was buying the Sabatini estate.

Their eyes met in the mirror.

'Will you zip me up?'

'Certo.'

'So tell me again,' she said, feeling his fingers brushing against her bare skin as he slid the zip of the close-fitting dress all the way up. 'The lawyer's name is Cristiano Branzi and his girlfriend is Nicoletta—'

'Ramelli.' There was a moment of hesitation and his eyes narrowed fractionally. 'And—just so you know—she and I used to have a thing a few years back.'

In the process of hooking in a dangly earring, Darcy's fingers stilled. 'A *thing*?'

'You really are going to have to stop looking so shocked, *cara*. I'm thirty-five years old and in Rome, as in all cities, social circles are smaller than you might imagine. She and I were lovers for a few months, that's all.'

That's all. Darcy's practised smile didn't waver. Just like her. Great sex for a few months and then goodbye—was that his usual pattern? Had Nicoletta been rewarded with a trip abroad just before the affair ended? But as she followed Renzo downstairs she was determined not to spoil their last evening and took the champagne Stefania offered, hoping she displayed more confidence than she felt as she rose to greet their guests.

Cristiano was a powerfully built man with piercing blue eyes and Darcy thought Nicoletta the most beautiful woman she'd ever seen. The Italian woman's sleek dark hair was swept up into a sophisticated chignon and she wore a dress which was obviously designer made. Real diamond studs glittered at her ears, echoing the smaller diamonds which sparkled in a watch which was slightly too loose for her narrow wrist. Darcy watched as she presented each smooth cheek in turn to be kissed by Renzo, wondering why she hadn't worn the turquoise dress after all. Why

hadn't she realised that of *course* the Italian woman
would also wear black, leaving the two of them wide
open for comparison? How cheap her own glimmering gown must seem in comparison—and how wild
her untameable red curls as they spilled down over
her shoulders towards breasts which were much too
large by fashionable standards.

'So...' Nicoletta smiled as they sat down to pro-
sciutto and slivers of iced melon at a candlelit table
decorated with roses. 'This is your first time in Italy,
Darcy?'

'It is,' answered Darcy, with a smile.

'But not your last, I hope?'

Darcy looked across the table at Renzo, thinking
it might bring the mood down if she suddenly an-
nounced that they were in the process of splitting up.

'Darcy isn't much of a traveller,' he said smoothly.

'Oh?'

Something made her say it. Was it bravado or stu-
pidity? Yet surely she wasn't *ashamed* of the person she really was. Not unless she honestly thought
she could compete with these glossy people, with
their Tuscan estates and diamond wristwatches which
probably cost as much as a small car.

'To be honest, I don't really have a lot of money to
go travelling.' She slanted Nicoletta a rueful smile.
'I'm a waitress.'

'A *waitress*?' Nicoletta's silver fork was returned
to her plate with a clatter, the dainty morsel she'd
speared remaining untouched. 'That is a very unusual
job.' There was a slightly perplexed pause. 'So how
did you and Renzo actually meet?'

Darcy registered the faint astonishment on Nicoletta's face, but what had she expected? And now she had dropped Renzo in it. He was probably going to bluster out some story about how he'd bumped into her in a bookshop or been introduced at a party by a friend of a friend. Except he'd told her very specifically that he didn't like lies, hadn't he?

'I met Darcy when she was working in a nightclub in London,' Renzo said. 'I walked in with some visiting colleagues and saw her serving cocktails to the people on the next table. She turned round and looked at me and that was it. I was completely blown away.'

'I'm not surprised,' murmured Cristiano. 'I have never seen hair as bright as yours before, Darcy. I believe this is what they call the show-stopping look?'

The compliment was unexpected and Darcy met Renzo's eyes, expecting to find mockery or anger in them but there was none. On the contrary, he looked as if he was *enjoying* the praise being directed at her and suddenly she wanted to turn and run from the room. Or tell him not to look at her that way because it was making her fantasise about a life which could never be hers.

She cleared her throat, trying to remember back to when she'd worked in that very hip restaurant which had been frequented by the media crowd. To remember how those high-profile people used to talk to each other when she arrived to offer them a bread roll, which they inevitably refused. They used to play everything down, didn't they? To act as if nothing really mattered.

'Oh, that's quite enough about me,' she said lightly. 'I'd much rather talk about Tuscany.'

'You like it here?' questioned Nicoletta. 'At Vallombrosa?'

'Who could fail to like it?' questioned Darcy simply. 'There can't be anywhere in the world as beautiful as this. The gardens are so lovely and the view is to die for.' She smiled as she reached for a piece of bread. 'If I had the money I'd snap it up in a shot. You're a very lucky man, Cristiano.'

'I'm very aware of that.' Cristiano's blue eyes crinkled. 'Nobody can quite believe that Renzo has put it on the market at last, after years of everyone offering him vast amounts of money to sell it. And he won't say what has suddenly changed his mind.'

But Darcy knew why. She'd seen the pain in his eyes when he'd talked about his parents' divorce and suspected his stepmother's death had made him want to let all that painful past go. He hadn't said that much but it surprised her that he'd confided in her at all. For a little while it had made her feel special—more than just his 'friend with benefits.' But that was fantasy, too. It was easy to share your secrets with someone you knew was planning to leave you.

Except for her, of course. She was one of those people whose secrets were just too dark to tell.

Course after course of delicious food was served—stuffed courgette flowers, ultra-fine pasta with softshell crab and a rich dessert of cherries and cream—all accompanied by fine wines from Renzo's cellar. Nicoletta skilfully fired a series of questions at her, some of which Darcy carefully avoided answering but fortunately Nicoletta enjoyed talking about herself much more. She waxed lyrical about her privileged upbringing in Parioli in Rome, her school in Switzerland and her fluency in four languages. It transpired that she had several dress shops in Rome, none of which she worked in herself.

'You should come visit, Darcy. Get Renzo to buy you something pretty.'

Darcy wondered if that was Nicoletta's way of subtly pointing out that the cheapness of her clothes hadn't gone unnoticed, but if it was, she didn't care. All she could think about right then was being alone with Renzo again as she tried not to focus on time slipping away from them. She returned to their room while he waved their guests goodbye and was naked in bed waiting for him when at last he came in and shut the door behind him.

'You were very good during dinner,' he said, unbuckling the belt of his trousers.

'Good? In what way?'

'A bewitching combination. A little defiant about your lowly job,' he observed as he stepped out of his boxer shorts. 'And there's no need to look at me that way, Darcy, because it's true. But your heartfelt praise about the property pleased Cristiano very much, though he's always been a sucker for a pretty girl. He's going to keep Gisella, Pasquale and Stefania on, by the way. He told me just before they left for Rome.'

'So all's well that ends well?' she questioned brightly.

'Who said anything about it ending?' he murmured, climbing into bed and pulling her into his arms so that she could feel the hard rod of his arousal pushing against her. 'I thought the night was only just beginning.'

They barely slept a wink. It was as if Renzo was determined to leave her with lasting memories of just what an amazing lover he was as he brought her to climax over and over again. As dawn coated the dark room with a pale daffodil light, Darcy found herself enjoying the erotic spectacle of Renzo's dark head between her thighs, gasping as his tongue cleaved over her exquisitely aroused flesh, until she quivered helplessly around him.

She was slow getting ready the next morning and when she walked into the dining room, Renzo glanced up from his newspaper.

'I need to leave for the airport soon,' she said.

'No, you don't. We'll fly back together on my jet,' he said, pouring her a cup of coffee.

Darcy sat down and reached for a sugar cube. *Start as you mean to go on. And remember that your future does not contain billionaire property tycoons with an endless supply of private transport.*

'Honestly, there's no need,' she said. 'I have a return ticket and I'm perfectly happy to go back on FlyCheap.'

The look he gave her was a mixture of wry, indulgent—but ultimately uncompromising. 'I'm not sending you back on a budget airline, Darcy. You're coming on my jet, with me.'

And if Darcy had thought that travelling in a chauffeur-driven car was the height of luxury, then flying in Renzo's private plane took luxury onto a whole new level. She saw the unmistakable looks of surprise being directed at her by two stewardesses as they were whisked through passport control at Florence airport. Were they thinking she didn't look like Renzo's usual *type*, with her cheap jewellery, her bouncing bosom and the fact that she was clearly out of her comfort zone?

But Darcy didn't care about that either. She was just going to revel in her last few hours with her lover and as soon as he'd dismissed the flight crew she unzipped his jeans. As she pulled down his silk boxers she realised this was the last time she would ever slide her lips over his rocky length and hear his helpless groan as he jerked inside her mouth. The last time he would ever give that low, growling moan as he clamped his hands possessively around her head to anchor her lips to the most sensitive part of his anatomy. Afterwards, he made love to her so slowly that she felt as if she would never come down to earth properly.

But all too soon the flight was over and they touched down in England where his car was waiting. Darcy hesitated as the driver held open the door for her.

'Could you drop me off at the Tube on the way?'

Renzo frowned, exasperation flattening his lips. 'Darcy, what is this? I'm not dropping you anywhere except home.'

'No. You don't have to do that.'

'I know I don't.' He paused before giving a flicker of a smile. 'You can even invite me in for coffee if you like.'

'Coffee?'

'There you go. You're sounding shocked again.' He shook his head. 'Isn't that what normally happens when a man takes a woman home after the kind of weekend we've just had? I've never even seen where you live.'

'I know you haven't. But you're not interested in my life. You've always made that perfectly clear.'

'Maybe I'm interested now,' he said stubbornly.

And now was too late, she thought. Why hadn't he done this at the beginning, when it might have meant something? He was behaving with all the predictability of a powerful man who had everything he wanted—his curiosity suddenly aroused by the one thing which was being denied him.

'It's small and cramped and all I can afford, which is why I'm moving to Norfolk,' she said defensively. 'It's about as far removed from where you live as it's possible to be and you'll hate it.'

'Why don't you let me be the judge of that? Unless you're ashamed of it, of course.'

Furiously, she glared at him. 'I'm not *ashamed* of it.'

'Well, then.' He shrugged. 'What's the problem?'

But Darcy's fingers were trembling as she unlocked her front door because she'd never invited *anyone* into this little sanctuary of hers. When you'd shared rooms and space for all of your life—when you'd struggled hard to find some privacy—then something which was completely your own became especially precious. 'Come in, then,' she said ungraciously.

Renzo stepped into the room and the first thing he noticed was that the living, dining and kitchen area were all crammed into the same space. And…his eyes narrowed…was that a narrow *bed* in the corner?

The second thing he noticed was how clean and unbelievably tidy it was—and the minimalist architect in him applauded her total lack of clutter. There

were no family photos or knick-knacks. The only em-
bellishment he could see was a cactus in a chrome pot
on the window sill and an art deco mirror, which reflected some much-needed extra light into the room.
And books. Lots of books. Whole lines of them,
neatly arranged in alphabetical order.

He turned to look at her. She had been careful
about sitting in the Tuscan sun but, even so, her fair
skin had acquired a faint glow. She looked much
healthier than she'd done when she'd arrived at Vallombrosa, that was for sure. In fact, she looked so
pretty in the yellow dress with blue flowers which she
had stubbornly insisted on laundering herself, that he
felt his heart miss a beat. And suddenly Renzo knew
he wasn't ready to let her go. Not yet. He thought
about the way she'd been in his arms last night. The
way they'd taken their coffee out onto the terrace at
Vallombrosa to stare at the moon, and he'd known a
moment of unexpected peace. Why end something
before it fizzled out all of its own accord, especially
when it still had the potential to give him so much
pleasure?

He glanced over towards her neat little kitchenette.
'So… Aren't you going to offer me coffee?'

'I've only got instant, I'm afraid.'

He did his best to repress a shudder. 'Just some
water, then.'

He watched as she poured him a glass of tap
water—he couldn't remember the last time he'd drunk
that—and added an ice cube. But when she put the
drink down on the table, he didn't touch it. Instead,
he fixed her with a steady gaze.

'I've had a good weekend,' he said slowly.

'Me, too. Actually, it was more than good.' She gave him a quick smile. 'Thank you.'

There was a pause. 'Look, this move to Norfolk seems a little…hasty. Why don't you stay in London a bit longer?'

'I told you why—and now you've seen for yourself my reasons. I want to start living differently.'

'I can understand that. But what if I told you I had an apartment you could use—somewhere much bigger and more comfortable than this? What then?'

'What, just like that? Let me guess.' Her emerald gaze bored into him. 'Even if you don't have one available, you'll magically "find" an apartment for me? Browse through your extensive property portfolio or have one of your staff discreetly rent somewhere? Thanks, but no, thanks. I'm not interested, Renzo. I have no desire to be a "kept woman" and fulfilling the stereotype of being a rich man's mistress, even if that's the way I'm currently heading.'

Her stubbornness infuriated him but it also produced another spark of admiration. How could a woman with so little be so proud and spirited and turn down an offer anyone else in her position would have leapt at? Renzo picked up the iced water and sipped it before walking over to the window and looking out at a red-brick wall. He wondered what it must be like to wake up to this view every morning, before putting on some drab uniform to spend the rest of the day carrying trays of food and drink.

He turned round. 'What if I asked you to delay going to Norfolk?'

She raised her eyebrows. 'And why would you do that?'

'Oh, come on, Darcy,' he said softly. 'You may have been an innocent when I bedded you, but you're not so innocent now. I have taught you a great deal—'

'Perhaps there's some kind of certificate I could nominate you for, if it's praise you're after?'

He gave a low laugh, turned on by an insolence he encountered from nobody else. He could see the wariness on her face as he took a step towards her, but he could also see the darkening of her eyes and the sudden stiffness of her body, as if she was using every bit of willpower not to give into what she really wanted. And Renzo knew enough about women to realise that this wasn't over. Not yet.

'It's not praise I want,' he said softly. 'It's you. I'm not ready to let you go.' He reached out to smooth down her riotous curls and felt the kick of lust as he pulled her into his arms. 'What if I told you that I liked the way you were with Cristiano and Nicoletta? That I find you charming in company as well as exquisite in bed and that maybe I'd like to take you out a little more. Why shouldn't we go to the theatre, or a party or two? Perhaps I've been a little selfish keeping you locked away and now I want to show you off to the world.'

'You make it sound as if I've passed some sort of hidden test!' she said indignantly.

'Maybe you have,' came his simple reply.

Darcy was torn, because his words were dangerous. She didn't want him *showing her off to the world*. What if someone remembered her? Someone who knew who she really was? And yet Renzo was only echoing the things she'd been thinking. Things she'd been trying and failing to deny—that she wasn't yet ready to walk away either.

'What if I gave you a key to my apartment?' His voice broke into her thoughts.

'A key?' she echoed.

'Why not? And—just so you know—I don't hand out keys every day of the week. Very few people are given access to my home because I value my privacy very highly.'

'So why me? To what do I owe this huge honour?'

'Because you've never asked me for anything,' he said quietly. 'And nobody's ever done that before.'

Darcy tried telling herself it was just another example of a powerful man being intrigued by the unfamiliar. But surely it was more than that. Wasn't the giving of a key—no matter how temporary—a sign that he *trusted* her? And wasn't trust the most precarious yet most precious thing in the world, especially considering Renzo's lack of it where women were concerned?

She licked her lips, tempted beyond reason, but really—when she stopped to think about it—what was holding her back? She'd escaped her northern life and left that dark world behind as she'd carved out a new identity for herself. She'd been completely underqualified and badly educated but night classes had helped make up for her patchy schooling—and her sunny disposition meant she'd been able to find waitressing work whenever she had put her mind to it. She wasn't quite sure where she wanted to be but she knew she was on her way. And who would possibly remember her after all this time? She'd left Manchester for London when she was sixteen and that was a long time ago. Didn't she deserve a little fun while she had the chance?

He was watching her closely and Darcy was savvy enough to realise her hesitation was turning him on. Yet she wasn't playing games with him. Her indecision was genuine. She really *was* trying to give him up, only it wasn't as easy as she'd imagined. She was beginning to suspect that Renzo Sabatini was becoming an addiction and that should have set off every alarm bell in her body because it didn't matter if it was drink or drugs or food—or in this case a man— addictions were dangerous. She knew that. Her personal history had taught her that in the bleakest way possible.

But now he was pulling her against him and she could feel all that hard promise shimmering beneath the surface of his muscular body. Enveloped by his arms, she found herself wanting to sink further into his powerful embrace, wanting to hold on to this brief sense of comfort and safety.

'Say yes, Darcy,' he urged softly, his breath warm against her lips. 'Take my key and be my lover for a little while longer.'

His hand was on her breast and her knees were starting to buckle and Darcy knew then that she wasn't going to resist him anytime soon.

'Okay,' she said, closing her eyes as he began to ruck up her dress. 'I'll stay for a bit longer.'

CHAPTER FIVE

THE LIMOUSINE SLID to a halt outside the Granchester Hotel as Renzo was caressing Darcy's thigh and he found himself thinking that she'd never looked more beautiful than she did tonight. Hungrily, he ran his gaze over the emerald shimmer of her gown, thinking that for once she looked like a billionaire's mistress.

He gave an almost imperceptive shake of his head. Didn't she realise that, despite her initial reluctance, she was entitled to a mistress's perks? He'd tried to persuade her that it would be easier all round if she enjoyed *all* the benefits of his wealth and made herself more available to him by giving up her lowly job, but she had stubbornly refused to comply. She'd told him he should be grateful she was no longer working in the nightclub and he had growled at the thought of her curvy body poured into that tight black satin while men drooled over her.

But tonight, a small victory had been won. For once she'd accepted his offer of a custom-made gown to wear to the prestigious ball he was holding in aid of his charity foundation, though it had taken some persuasion. His mouth flattened because where once her stubborn independence had always excited him, her independence was starting to rankle, as was her determination to carry on waiting tables even though it took up so much of her time.

'The princess is supposed to be smiling when she goes to the ball,' he observed wryly, feeling her sequin-covered thigh tense beneath his fingers. 'Not looking as if she's walking towards her own execution.'

'But I'm not a princess, Renzo. I'm a waitress who happens to be wearing a gown which cost as much as I earn in three months.' She touched her fingertips to one of the mother-of-pearl clips which gleamed like milky rainbows against the abundant red curls. 'If you must know, I feel like Cinderella.'

'Ah, but the difference is that your clothes will not turn into rags at midnight, *cara*. When the witching hour comes you will be doing something far more pleasurable than travelling home in a pumpkin. So wipe that concerned look from your face and give me that beautiful smile instead.'

Feeling like a puppet, Darcy did as he asked, flashing a bright grin as someone rushed forward to open the car door for her. Carefully, she picked up the fishtail skirt of her emerald gown and stepped onto the pavement in her terrifyingly high shoes, thinking how quickly you could get used to being driven around like this and having people leap to attention simply because you were in the company of one of the world's most powerful men. What was not so easy was getting rid of the growing feeling of anxiety which had been gnawing away inside her for weeks now—a sick, queasy feeling which just wouldn't shift.

Because she was starting to realise that she was

stuck. Stuck in some awful limbo. Living in a strange, parallel world which wasn't real and locked into it by her inability to walk away from the only man who had ever been able to make her feel like a real woman.

The trouble was that things had changed and they were changing all the time. Why hadn't she realised that agreeing to accept the key to his apartment would strengthen the connection between them and make it even harder for her to sever her ties with him? It had made things…*complicated*. She didn't want her heart to thunder every time she looked at him or her body to melt with instant desire. Her worst fears had been realised and Renzo Sabatini had become her addiction. She ran her tongue over her lips. She knew he was bad for her yet she couldn't seem to give him up.

Sometimes she found herself longing for him to tire of her and kick *her* out since she didn't have the strength to end it herself. Wouldn't such a move force her to embrace the new life in Norfolk which she'd done absolutely nothing about—not since the day he'd given her his key and then made her come on the narrow bed in her humble bedsit, which these days she only ever visited when Renzo was away on business?

She could hear him telling his driver to take the rest of the night off and that they'd get a taxi home when the ball was over and she wished he wouldn't be so thoughtful with his staff. No wonder they all thought the world of him. But Darcy didn't need any more reasons to like him. Hadn't it been easier not to let her heart become involved when their affair had been more low-key, rather than this new-found openness with trips to the opera and theatre and VIP balls?

And now he was taking her arm and leading her towards the red-carpeted marble staircase where the paparazzi were clustered. She'd known they were going to be there, but had also known she couldn't possibly avoid them. And anyway, they weren't going to be looking at *her* They would be far too busy focussing on the Hollywood actress who was wearing the most revealing dress Darcy had ever seen, or the married co-star she was rumoured to be having an affair with.

Flashbulbs exploded to light up the warm night and although Darcy quickly tried to turn her head away, the press weren't having any of it. And wasn't that a TV camera zooming in on her? She wondered why she had let the dress designer put these stupid clips in her hair which meant she couldn't hide behind the usual comforting curtain of her curls. This was the most high-profile event they'd attended as a couple but there had been no way of getting out of it—not when it was Renzo's foundation and he was the man who'd organised it.

She felt like a fox on the run as they entered the ballroom but the moment she was swallowed up by all that glittering splendour, she calmed down. The gilded room had been decked out with giant sprays of pink-and-white cherry blossoms, symbolising the hope which Renzo's foundation brought to suffering children in war-torn areas of the world. Tall, guttering candles gave the place a fairy-tale feel. On a raised dais, a string quartet was playing and the exquisitely dressed guests were mingling in small chattering groups. It was the fanciest event she'd ever attended and dinner had been prepared by a clutch of award-winning chefs. But the moment the first rich course was placed in front of her, Darcy's stomach did an intricate kind of twist, which meant she merely pushed the food around her plate and tried not to look at it. At least Renzo didn't notice or chide her for her lack of appetite as he might normally have done—he was too busy talking to fundraisers and donors and being photographed next to the diamond necklace which was the star lot for the night's auction.

But after disappearing into one of the restrooms, where a splash of her face with cold water made her queasiness shift, Darcy became determined to enjoy herself. *Stop living so fearfully*, she chided herself as she chatted attentively whenever she was introduced to someone new and rose eagerly to her feet when Renzo asked her to dance. And that bit felt like heaven. His cheek was warm against hers and her body fitted so snugly into his that she felt like one of those salt and pepper shakers you sometimes found in old-fashioned tea rooms—as if they were made to be together. But they weren't. Of course they weren't.

She knew this couldn't continue. She'd been seduced into staying but if she stayed much longer she was going to have to tell him the truth. Open up about her past. Confess to being the daughter of a junkie and all the other stuff which went with it. He would probably end their affair immediately and a swift, clean cut might just be the best thing. She would be heartbroken for a while of course, but she would get over it because you could get over just about anything if you worked at it. It would be better than forcing herself to walk away and having to live with the stupid spark of hope that maybe it *could* have worked.

'So… How is the most beautiful woman in the

room?' He bent his head to her ear. 'You seem to be enjoying yourself.'

She closed her eyes and inhaled his sultry masculine scent. 'I am.'

'Not as bad as you thought it was going to be?'

'Not nearly so bad.'

'Think you might like to come to something like this again in the future?'

'I *could* be persuaded.'

He smiled. 'Then let's go and sit down. The auction is about to begin.'

The auctioneer stepped onto the stage and began to auction off the different lots which had been donated as prizes. A holiday in Mauritius, a box at the opera and a tour of Manchester United football ground all went under the hammer for eye-watering amounts, and then the diamond necklace was brought out to appreciative murmurs.

Darcy listened as the bidding escalated, only vaguely aware of Renzo lifting a careless finger from time to time. But suddenly everyone was clapping and looking at *them* and she realised that Renzo had successfully bid for the necklace and the auctioneer's assistant had handed it to him and he was putting it on *her* neck. She was aware of every eye in the room on them as he fixed the heavy clasp in place and she was aware of the dazzle of the costly gems.

'In truth you should wear emeralds to match your eyes,' he murmured. 'But since diamonds were the only thing on offer they will have to do. What do you think, *cara*?'

Darcy couldn't get rid of the sudden lump in her throat. It felt like a noose. The stones were heavy and the metal was cold. But there was no time to protest because cameras were flashing again and this time they were all directed at her. Sweat beaded her forehead and she felt dizzy, only able to breathe normally when the rumour went round that the Hollywood star was exiting through the kitchens and the press pack left the ballroom to follow her.

Darcy turned to Renzo, her fingertips touching the unfamiliar stones. 'You do realise I can't possibly accept this?' she questioned hoarsely.

'And you do realise that I am not going to let you give it back? Your tastes are far too modest for a woman in your position. You are the lover of a very wealthy man, Darcy, and I want you to wear it. I want you to have some pretty jewels for all the pleasure you've given me.'

His voice had dipped into a silken caress, which usually would have made her want to melt, but he made it sound like payment for services rendered. Was that how he saw it? Darcy's smile felt as if someone had stitched it onto her face with a rusty needle. Shouldn't she at least try to look as a woman *should* look when a man had just bought something this valuable? And wasn't she in danger of being a hypocrite? After all, she had a key to his Belgravia home—wasn't that just a short step to accepting his jewels? What about the designer dress she was wearing tonight, and the expensive shoes? He'd bought those for her, hadn't he?

Something like fear clutched at her heart and she knew she couldn't put it off any longer. She was going to have to come clean about her mum and the children's home and all the other sordid stuff.

So tell him. Explain your aversion to accepting gifts and bring this whole crazy relationship to a head, because at least that will end the uncertainty and you'll know where you stand.

But in the car he kissed her and when they reached the apartment he kissed her some more, unclipping the diamond choker and dropping it onto a table in the sitting room as casually as if it had been made of paste. His hands were trembling as he undressed her and so were hers. He made love to her on one of the sofas and then he carried her into the bedroom and did it all over again—and who would want to talk about the past at a moment like that?

They made love most of the night and because she'd asked for a day off after the ball, Darcy slept late next morning. When she eventually woke, it was getting on for noon and Renzo had left for the office long ago. *And still she hadn't told him.* She showered and dressed but her queasiness had returned and she could only manage some mint tea for breakfast. The morning papers had been delivered and, with a growing sense of nervousness, she flicked through the pages until she found the column which listed society events. And there she was in all her glory—in her mermaid dress of green sequins, the row of fiery white diamonds glittering at her throat, with Renzo standing just behind her, a hint of possessiveness in the sexy smile curving his lips.

She stood up abruptly, telling herself she was being paranoid. Who was going to see, or, more important, to *care* that she was in the wretched paper?

The morning slipped away. She went for a walk, bought a bag of oranges to put through the squeezer and was just nibbling on a piece of dry toast when the doorbell rang and Darcy frowned. It never rang when Renzo wasn't here—and not just because his wasn't a lifestyle where people made spontaneous visits. He'd meant what he said about guarding his privacy; his home really was his fortress. People just didn't come round.

She pressed the button on the intercom.

'Yes?'

'Is that Darcy Denton?' It was a male voice with a broad Manchester accent.

'Who is this?' she questioned sharply.

'An old friend of yours.' There was a pause. 'Drake Bradley.'

For a minute Darcy thought she might pass out. She thought about pretending to be someone else— the housekeeper perhaps. Or just cutting the connection while convincing herself that she didn't have to speak to anyone—let alone Drake Bradley. But the bully who had ruled the roost in the children's home had never been the kind of person to take no for an answer. If she refused to speak to him she could imagine him settling down to wait until Renzo got home and she just imagined what he might have to say to him. Shivering, she stared at her pale reflection in the hall mirror. What was it they said? Keep your friends close but your enemies closer.

'What do you want?'

'Just a few minutes of your time. Surely you can spare that, Darcy.'

Telling herself it was better to brazen it out, Darcy pressed the buzzer, her heart beating out a primitive tattoo as she opened the door to find Drake standing there—a sly expression on his pockmarked face. A decade had made his hair recede, but she would have recognised him immediately and her blood ran cold as the sight of him took her back to a life she'd thought she'd left for ever.

'What do you want?' she asked again.

'That's not much of a welcome, is it? What's the matter, Darcy? Aren't you going to invite me in? Surely you're not ashamed of me?'

But the awful thing was that she *was*. She'd moved on a lot since that turbulent period when their lives had merged and clashed, yet Drake looked as if he'd been frozen in time. Wearing clothes which swamped his puny frame, he had oil beneath his fingernails and on the fingers of his left hand were the letters *H*, *A*, *T*, *E*. *You have no right to judge him*, she told herself. He was simply another survivor from the shipwreck of their youth. Surely she owed him a little hospitality when she'd done so well for herself.

She could smell stale tobacco and the faint underlying odour of sweat as she opened the door wider and he brushed past her. He followed her into the enormous sitting room and she wondered if he was seeing the place as she had seen it the first time she'd been here, when she'd marvelled at the space and light and cleanliness. And, of course, the view.

'Wow.' He pursed his lips together and whistled as he stared out at the whispering treetops of Eaton Square. 'You've certainly landed on your feet, Darcy.'

'Are you going to tell me why you're here?'

His weasel eyes narrowed. 'Not even going to offer me a drink? It's a hot day outside. I could murder a drink.'

Darcy licked her lips. *Don't aggravate him. Tolerate him for a few minutes and then he'll go.* 'What would you like?'

'Got a beer?'

'Sure.'

Her underlying nausea seemed to intensify as Darcy went to the kitchen to fetch him a beer. When she returned he refused her offer of a glass and began to glug greedily from the bottle.

'How did you find me?' she asked, once he had paused long enough to take a breath.

He put the bottle down on a table. 'Saw you on the news last night, walking into that big hotel. Yeah. On TV. Couldn't believe my eyes at first. I thought to myself, that can't be Darcy Denton—daughter of one of Manchester's best known hookers. Not on the arm of some rich dude like Sabatini. So I headed along to the hotel to see for myself and hung around until your car arrived. I'm good at hanging around in the shadows, I am.' He smiled slyly. 'I overheard your man giving the address to the taxi driver so I thought I'd come and pay you a visit to catch up on old times. See for myself how you've come up in the world.'

Darcy tried to keep her voice light. To act as if her heart weren't pounding so hard it felt as if it might burst right out of her chest. 'You still haven't told me what you want.'

His smile grew calculating. 'You've landed on your feet, Darcy. Surely it's no big deal to help out an old friend?'

'Are you asking for money?' she said.

He sneered. 'What do you think?'

She thought plenty but nothing she'd want *him* to

hear. She thought about how much cash she had squirrelled away in her bank account. She'd amassed funds since she'd been with Renzo because he wouldn't let her pay for anything. *But it was still a pitiful amount by most people's standards, and besides...if you gave in to blackmail once then you opened up the floodgates.*

And she didn't need to give into blackmail because hadn't she already decided to tell Renzo about her past? This might be the push she needed to see if he still wanted her when he discovered who she really was. Her mouth dried. Dared she take that risk?

She had no choice.

Drawing her shoulders back, she looked straight into Drake's shifty eyes. 'You're not getting any money from me,' she said quietly. 'I'd like you to leave and not bother coming back.'

His lip curled and then he shrugged. 'Have it your own way, Darcy.'

Of course, if she'd thought it through properly, she might have wondered why he obeyed her quite so eagerly...

Renzo's eyes narrowed as the man with the pock-marked face shoved his way past, coming out of *his* private elevator as if he had every right to do so. His frown deepened. Had he been making some kind of delivery? Surely not, dressed like *that*? He stood for a moment watching his retreating back, instinct alerting him to a danger he didn't quite understand. But it was enough to cast a shadow over a deliciously high mood which had led to him leaving work early—

something which had caused his secretary to blink at him in astonishment.

In truth, Renzo had been pretty astonished himself. Taking a half-day off wasn't the way he usually operated, but he had wanted to spend the rest of the afternoon with Darcy. Getting into bed with her. Running his fingers through her silky riot of curls. Losing himself deep in her tight, tight body with his mouth on her breast. Maybe even telling her how good she made him feel. Plus he'd received an urgent message reminding him that he needed to insure the necklace he'd spent a fortune on last night.

After watching the man leave the building, Renzo took the penthouse elevator where the faint smell of tobacco and beer still tainted the air. He unlocked the door to his apartment just as Darcy tore out of the sitting room. But the trouble was she didn't look like the Darcy of this morning's smouldering fantasies, when somehow he'd imagined arriving home to see her clad in that black satin basque and matching silk stockings he'd recently bought. Not only was she wearing jeans and a baggy shirt—her face was paler than usual and her eyes looked huge and haunted with something which looked like guilt. Now, why was that? he wondered.

'Renzo!' she exclaimed, raking a handful of bouncing red curls away from her forehead and giving him an uncertain smile. 'I wasn't expecting you.'

'So I see.' He put his briefcase on the hall table. 'Who was the man I saw leaving?'

'The man?' she questioned, but he could hear the sudden quaver in her voice.

Definitely guilt, he thought grimly.

'The man I met coming down in the elevator. Bad skin. Bad smell. Who was he, Darcy?'

Darcy met the cool accusation in Renzo's eyes and knew she had run out of reasons not to tell him.

'I need to talk to you,' she said.

He didn't respond straight away, just walked into the sitting room leaving her to follow him, her senses alerted to the sudden tension in his body and the forbidding set of his shoulders. Usually, he pulled her into his arms and kissed all the breath out of her when he arrived home but today he hadn't even touched her. And when he turned around, Darcy was shocked by the cold expression on his face.

'So talk,' he said.

She felt like someone who'd been put on stage in front of a vast audience and told to play a part she hadn't learnt. Because she'd never spoken about this before, not to anyone. She'd buried it so deep it was almost inaccessible. But she needed to access it now, before his irritation grew any deeper.

'He's someone I was in care with.'

'In care?'

She nodded. 'That's what they call it in England, although it's a bit of a misnomer because you don't actually get much in the way of care. I lived in a children's home in the north for most of my childhood.'

His black eyes narrowed. 'What happened to your parents?'

Darcy could feel a bead of sweat trickling its way down her back. Here it was. The question which separated most normal people from the unlucky few. The question which made you feel a freak no matter which way you answered it. Was it any wonder she'd spent her life trying to avoid having to do so?

And yet didn't it demonstrate the shallowness of her relationship with Renzo that in all the time she'd known him—this was the first time he'd actually asked? Dead parents had been more than enough information for him. He hadn't been the type of person to quiz her about her favourite memory or how she'd spent her long-ago Christmases.

'I'm illegitimate,' she said baldly. 'I don't know who my father was and neither did my mother. And she… Well, for a lot of my childhood, she wasn't considered fit to be able to take care of me.'

'Why not?'

'She had…' She hesitated. 'She had a drug problem. She was a junkie.'

He let out a long breath and Darcy found herself searching his face for some kind of understanding, some shred of compassion for a situation which had been out of her control. But his expression remained like ice. His black eyes were stony as they skimmed over her, looking at her as if it was the first time he'd seen her and not liking what they saw.

'Why didn't you tell me any of this before?'

'Because you didn't ask. And you didn't ask because you didn't want to know!' she exclaimed. 'You made that very clear. We haven't had the kind of relationship where we talked about stuff like this. You just wanted…sex.'

She waited for him to deny it. To tell her that there had been more to it than that—and Darcy realised she was already thinking of their relationship in the past tense. But he didn't deny it. His sudden closed look made his features appear shuttered as he walked over to the table near where he'd undressed her last night and her heart missed a beat as she saw him looking down at the polished surface, on which stood a lamp and nothing else.

Nothing else.

It took a moment for her to register the significance of this and that moment came when he lifted his black gaze to hers and slanted her an unfathomable look. 'Where's the necklace?' he questioned softly.

Darcy's mind raced. In the heat of everything that had happened, she'd forgotten about the diamond necklace he'd bought last night for her at the auction. She vaguely remembered the dazzle of the costly gems as he'd dropped them onto the table, but his hands had been all over her at the time and it had blotted out everything except the magic of his touch. Had she absent-mindedly tidied it away when she was picking up her clothes this morning? No. It had definitely been there when...

Fear and horror clamped themselves around her suddenly racing heart.

When...

Drake! Her throat dried as she remembered leaving him alone in the room while she went to fetch him a beer. Remembered the way he'd hurriedly left after his half-hearted attempt at blackmail. Had Drake stolen the necklace?

Of course he had.

'I don't—'

His voice was like steel. 'Did your friend take it?'

'He's not—'

'What's the matter, Darcy?' Contemptuously, he

cut through her protest. 'Did I arrive home unexpectedly and spoil your little plan?'

'What *plan*?'

'Oh, come on. Isn't this what's known in the trade as a scam? To rob me. To cheat on me.'

Darcy stared at him in disbelief. 'You can't honestly believe that?'

'Can't I? Perhaps it's the first clear-headed thought I've had in a long time, now that I'm no longer completely mesmerised by your pale skin and witchy eyes.' He shook his head like a man who was emerging from a deep coma. 'Now I'm beginning to wonder whether something like this was in your sights all along.'

Darcy felt foreboding icing her skin. 'What are you talking about?' she whispered.

'I've often wondered,' he said harshly, 'what you might give a man who has everything. Another house, or a faster car?' He shook his head. 'No. Material wealth means nothing when you have plenty. But innocence—ah! Now that is a very different thing.'

'You're not making sense.'

'Think about it. What is a woman's most prized possession, *cara mia*?' The Italian words of endearment dripped like venom from his lips. '*Sì*. I can see from your growing look of comprehension that you are beginning to understand. Her virginity. Precious and priceless and the biggest bartering tool in the market. And hasn't it always been that way?'

'Renzo.' She could hear the desperation in her voice now but she couldn't seem to keep it at bay. 'You don't mean that.'

'Sometimes I would ask myself,' he continued,

still in that same flat tone, 'why someone as beautiful and sensual as you—someone hard-up and working in a dead-end job—hadn't taken a rich lover to catapult herself out of her poverty before I came along.'

Desperation morphed into indignation. 'You mean...use a man as a meal ticket?'

'Why are you looking so shocked—or is that simply an expression you've managed to perfect over the years? Isn't that what every woman does ultimately—feed like a leech off a man?' His black gaze roved over her. 'But not you. At least, not initially. Did you decide to deny yourself pleasure— to look at the long game rather than the lure of instant gratification? To hold out for the richest man available, who just happened to be me—someone who was blown away by your extraordinary beauty coupled with an innocence I'd never experienced before?' He gave a cynical smile. 'But you were cunning, too. I see that now. For a cynic like me, a spirited show of independence was pretty much guaranteed to wear me down. So you refused my gifts. You bought cheap clothes and budget airline tickets while valiantly offering me the money you'd saved. What a touching gesture—the hard-up waitress offering the jaded architect a handful of cash. And I fell for it—hook, line and sinker! I was sucked in by your stubbornness and your pride.'

'It wasn't like that!' she defended fiercely.

'You must have thought you'd hit the jackpot when I gave you the key to my flat and bought you a diamond necklace,' he bit out. 'Just as I did when you gave yourself so willingly to me and I discovered you were a virgin. I allowed my ego to be flattered and to blind myself to the truth. How could I have *been* so blind?'

Darcy felt her head spin and that horrible queasy feeling came washing over her again, in giant waves. This couldn't be happening. In a minute she would wake up and the nightmare would be over. But it wouldn't, would it? She was living her nightmare and the proof was right in front of her eyes. In the midst of her confusion and hurt she saw the look of something like satisfaction on Renzo's face. She remembered him mentioning his parents' divorce and how bitterly he'd said that women could never be trusted. Was he somehow pleased that his prejudices had been reinforced and he could continue thinking that way? Yes, he was, she realised. He *wanted* to believe badly of her.

She made one last attempt because wasn't there still some tiny spark of hope which existed—a part which didn't want to let him go? 'None of that—'

'Save your lying words because I don't want to hear them. You're only upset because I came home early and found you out. How were you going to explain the absence of the necklace, Darcy?' he bit out. 'A "burglary" while you were out shopping? Shifting the blame onto one of the people who service these apartments?'

'You think I'd be capable of that?'

'I don't know what you're capable of, do I?' he said coldly. 'I just want you to listen to what I'm going to say. I'm going out and by the time I get back I want you out of here. Every last trace of you. I don't ever want to see your face again. Understand? And for what it's worth—and I'm sure you realise it's a lot— you can keep the damned necklace.'

'You're not going to go to the police?'

'And advertise exactly what kind of woman my girlfriend really is and the kind of low-life company she keeps? That wouldn't exactly do wonders for my reputation, would it? Do whatever you'd planned to do with it all along.' He paused and his mouth tightened as his black gaze swept down over her body. 'Think of it as payment for services rendered. A clean-break pay-off, if you like.'

It was the final straw. Nausea engulfed her. She could feel her knees buckling and a strange roaring in her head. Her hand reached out to grab at the nearest chair but she missed and Darcy felt herself sliding helplessly to the ground, until her cheek was resting on the smooth silk of the Persian rug and her eyes were level with his ankles and the handmade Italian shoes which swum in and out of focus.

His voice seemed to come from a long way off. 'And you can spare me the histrionics, Darcy. They won't make me change my mind.'

'Who's asking you to change your mind?' she managed, from beneath gritted teeth.

She saw his shadow move as he stepped over her and a minute later she heard the sound of the front door slamming shut.

And after that, thankfully, she passed out.

CHAPTER SIX

'YOU CAN'T GO ON like this, Darcy, you really can't.'

The midwife sounded both kind and stern and Darcy was finding it difficult keeping her lips from wobbling. Because stern she could handle. Stern was something she was used to. It was the kindness which got to her every time, which made her want to cover her face with her hands and howl like a wounded animal. And she couldn't afford to break down, because if she did—she might never put herself back together again.

Her hand slipped down to her belly. 'You're sure my baby's okay?' she questioned for the fourth time.

'Your baby's fine. Take a look at the scan and see. A little bit on the small side perhaps, but thriving. Unlike you. You're wearing yourself out,' continued the midwife, a frown creasing her plump face. 'You're working too hard and not eating properly, by the look of you.'

'Honestly, I'll try harder. I'll…I'll cut down on my hours at work and start eating more vegetables,' said Darcy as she rolled up her sleeve. And she would. She would do whatever it took because all she could think about was that her baby was safe. *Safe.* Relief washed over her in almost tangible waves as the terror she'd experienced during that noisy ambulance ride began to recede. 'Does that mean I can go home?'

'I wanted to talk to you about that. I'm not very happy about letting you go anywhere,' said the midwife. 'Unless you've got somebody who can be there for you.'

Darcy tried not to flinch. She supposed she could pretend she had a caring mother or protective sister or even—ha, ha, ha—a loving husband. But that would be irresponsible. Because it wasn't just her she was looking out for any more. There was a baby growing inside her. Her throat constricted. Renzo's baby.

She tried not to tense up as the midwife began to measure her blood pressure. Things hadn't been easy since Renzo had left her lying on the floor of his Belgravia apartment, accusing her of histrionics before slamming the door behind him. But Darcy's unexpected faint hadn't been caused by grief or anger, though it had taken a couple of weeks more to realise why a normally healthy young woman should have passed out for no apparent reason. It was when she'd found herself retching in the bathroom that she'd worked it out for herself. And then, of course, she wondered how she could have been so stupid to have not seen it before. It all added up. But her general queasiness and lack of appetite—even the lateness of her period—had been easy to overlook after Renzo had dumped her.

Of course she'd hoped. Hoped like mad she'd somehow got her dates muddled, but deep down she'd known she hadn't because the brand-new aching in her breasts had told her so. She'd gone out to buy a pregnancy kit and the result had come as a shock but no great surprise. Heart racing, she'd sat on the floor of her bathroom in Norfolk staring at the blue line, wondering who to tell. But even if she *had* made some friends in her new home town, she knew there was only one person she *could* tell. Tears of injustice had stung her eyes. The man who thought she was a thief and a con woman. Who had looked at her with utter contempt in his eyes. But that was irrelevant. Renzo's opinion of her didn't really matter—all that mattered was that she let him know he was going to be a father.

If only it had been that easy. Every call she'd made had gone straight through to voicemail and she'd been reluctant to leave him her news in a message. So she'd telephoned his office and been put through to one of his secretaries for another humiliating experience. She'd felt as if the woman was reading from a script as she'd politely told her that Signor Sabatini was unavailable for the foreseeable future. She remembered the beads of sweat which had broken out on her forehead as she'd asked his secretary to have him ring her back. And her lack of surprise when he hadn't.

'Why…?' Her voice faltered as she looked up into the midwife's lined face. 'Why do I have to have someone at home with me?'

'Because twenty-eight weeks is a critical time in a woman's pregnancy and you need to take extra care. Surely there must be someone you could ask. Who's the baby's father, Darcy?'

Briefly, Darcy closed her eyes. So this was it. The point where she really needed to be self-sacrificing and ignore pride and ego and instinct. For the first time in a long time images of Renzo's darkly rugged face swam into her mind, because she'd been trying her best not to think about him. To forget that chiselled jaw and lean body and the way he used to put on those sexy, dark-rimmed glasses while he was working on plans for one of his buildings. To a large extent she had succeeded in forgetting him, banishing memories of how it used to feel to wake up in his arms, as she concentrated on her new job at the local café.

But now she must appeal for help from the man who had made her feel so worthless—whose final gesture had taken her back to those days when people used to look down their noses at her and not believe a word she said. She told herself it didn't matter what Renzo thought when the hospital phoned him. That she didn't care if he considered her a no-good thief because she knew the truth and that was all that mattered. Her hand reached down to lie protectively over her belly, her fingers curving over its hard swell. She would do anything to protect the life of this unborn child.

Anything.

And right at the top of that list was the need to be strong. She'd been strong at the beginning of the affair and it had protected her against pain. She'd done her usual thing of keeping her emotions on ice and had felt good about herself. Even during that weekend when he'd taken her to Tuscany and hinted at his trust issues and the fickleness of women, she had still kept her feelings buried deep. She hadn't expected anything—which was why it had come as such a surprise to her when they'd got back to England and he'd offered her the key to his apartment.

Had that been when she'd first let her guard down

and her feelings had started to change? Or had she just got carried away with her new position in life? Her plans to move to Norfolk had been quietly shelved because she'd enjoyed being his mistress, hadn't she? She'd enjoyed going to that fancy ball with him, when—after her initial flurry of nerves—she'd waltzed in that cherry blossom–filled ballroom in his arms. And if things hadn't gone so badly wrong and Drake hadn't turned up, it probably wouldn't have taken long for her to get used to wearing Renzo's jewels either.

She'd been a fool and it was time to stop acting like a fool.

Never again would she be whimpering Darcy Denton, pleading with her cruel Italian lover to believe her. He could think what the hell he liked as long as he helped take care of her baby.

She opened her eyes and met the questioning look in the midwife's eyes.

'His name is Renzo Sabatini,' she said.

Feeling more impotent than he'd felt in years, Renzo paced up and down the sterile hospital corridor, oblivious to the surreptitious looks from the passing nurses. For a man unused to waiting, he couldn't believe he was being forced to bide his time until the ward's official visiting hours and he got the distinct impression that any further pleas to be admitted early would by vetoed by the dragon-like midwife he'd spoken to earlier, who had made no secret of her disapproval. With a frown on her face she'd told him that his girlfriend was overworked and underfed and clearly on the breadline. Her gaze had swept over him, taking in his dark suit, silk tie and handmade Italian shoes and he could see from her eyes that she was sizing up his worth. He was being judged, he realised—and he didn't like to be judged. Nor put in the role of an absentee father-to-be who refused to accept his responsibilities.

But amid all this confusion was a shimmering of something he couldn't understand, an emotion which licked like fire over his cold heart and was confusing the life out of him. Furiously, he forced himself to concentrate on facts. To get his head around the reason he was here—why he'd been driven to some remote area of Norfolk on what had felt like the longest journey of his life. And then he needed to decide what he was going to do about it. His head spun as his mind went over and over the unbelievable fact.

Darcy was going to have a baby.

His baby.

His mouth thinned.

Or so she said.

Eventually he was shown into the side room of a ward where she lay on a narrow hospital bed—her bright hair the only thing of colour in an all-white environment. Her face was as bleached as the bed sheets and her eyes were both wary and hostile as she looked at him. He remembered the last time he'd seen her. When she'd slid to the floor and he had just let her lie there and now his heart clenched with guilt because she looked so damned fragile lying propped up against that great bank of pillows.

'Darcy,' he said carefully.

She looked as if she had been sucking on a lemon as she spoke. 'You came.'

'I had no choice.'

'Don't lie,' she snapped. 'Of course you did! You could have just ignored the call from the hospital, just like you've ignored all my other calls up until now.'

He wanted to deny it but how could he when it was true? 'Yes,' he said flatly. 'I could.'

'You let my calls go through to voicemail,' she accused.

Letting out a breath, Renzo slowly nodded. At the time it had seemed the only sane solution. He hadn't wanted to risk speaking to her, because hadn't he worried he would cave in and take her back, even if it was for only one night? Because after she'd gone he hadn't been able to forget her as easily as he'd imagined, even though she had betrayed his trust in her. Even when he thought about the missing diamonds and the way she'd allowed that creep to enter his home—that still didn't erase her from his mind. He'd started to wonder whether he'd made a big mistake and whether he should give her another chance, but pride and a tendency to think the worst about women had stopped him acting on it. He'd known that 50 per cent of relationships didn't survive—so why go for one which had the odds stacked against it from the start? Yet she'd flitted in and out of his mind in a way which no amount of hard work or travelling had been able to fix.

'Guilty as charged,' he said evenly.

'And you told your secretary not to put me through to you.'

'She certainly would have put you through if she'd known the reason you were ringing. Why the hell didn't you tell her?'

'Are you out of your mind? Is that how you like to see your women, Renzo?' she demanded. 'To have them plead and beg and humiliate themselves? *Yes, I know he doesn't want to speak to me, but could you please tell him I'm expecting his baby?* Or would you rather I had hung around outside the Sabatini building, waiting for the big boss to leave work so I could grab your elbow and break my news to you on a busy London street? Maybe I should have gone to the papers and sold them a story saying that my billionaire boyfriend was denying paternity!'

'Darcy,' he said, and now his voice had gentled. 'I'm sorry I accused you of stealing the necklace.'

Belligerently, she raised her chin. 'Just not sorry enough to seek me out to tell me that before?'

He thought how tough she was—with a sudden inner steeliness which seemed so at odds with her fragile exterior. 'I jumped to the wrong conclusions,' he said slowly, 'because I'm very territorial about my space.' But he had been territorial about her, too, hadn't he? And old-fashioned enough to want to haul that complete stranger up against the wall and demand to know what he'd been doing alone with her. 'Look, this isn't getting us anywhere. You shouldn't be getting distressed.'

'What, in my *condition*?'

'Yes. Exactly that. In your condition. You're pregnant.' The unfamiliar word sounded foreign on his lips and once again he felt the lick of something painful in his heart. She looked so damned vulnerable lying there that his instinct was to take her in his arms and cradle her—if the emerald blaze in her eyes weren't defying him to dare try. 'The midwife says you need somebody to take care of you.'

Darcy started biting her lip, terrified that the stupid tears pricking at the backs of her eyes would start pouring down her cheeks. She hated the way this newfound state of hers was making her emotions zigzag all over the place, so she hardly recognised herself any more. She was supposed to be staying strong only it wasn't easy when Renzo was sounding so...*protective*. His words were making her yearn for something she'd never had, nor expected to have. She found herself looking up into his darkly handsome face and a wave of longing swept over her. She wanted to reach out her arms and ask him to hold her. She wanted him to keep her safe.

And she had to stop thinking that way. It wasn't a big deal that he'd apologised for something he needed to apologise for. She needed to remind herself that Renzo Sabatini wouldn't even *be* here if it weren't for the baby.

'It's the unborn child which needs taking care of,' she said coldly. 'Not me.'

His gaze drifted down to the black-and-white image which was lying on top of the locker. 'May I?'

She shrugged, trying to ignore the tug at her heart as he picked it up to study it, as engrossed as she had ever seen him. 'Suit yourself.'

And when at last he raised his head and looked at her, there was a look on his face she'd never seen before. Was that wonder or joy which had transformed his dark and shuttered features?

'It's a boy,' he said slowly.

She'd forgotten about his precise eye and attention

to detail, instantly able to determine the sex of the baby where most men might have seen nothing but a confusing composition of black and white.

'It is,' she agreed.

'A son,' he said, looking down at it again.

The possessive way his voice curled round the word scared her. It took her back to the days when she'd been hauled in front of social services who'd been trying to place her in a stable home. Futile attempts which had lasted only as long as it took her mother to discover her new address and turn up on the doorstep at midnight, high on drugs and demanding money in 'payment' for her daughter. What had those interviews taught her? That you should confront the great big elephant in the room, instead of letting it trample over you when you weren't looking.

'Aren't you going to ask whether it's yours?' she said. 'Isn't that what usually happens in this situation?'

He lifted his gaze and now his eyes were flinty. 'Is it?'

Angered by the fact he'd actually *asked* despite her having pushed him into it, Darcy hesitated—tempted by a possibility which lay before her. If she told him he wasn't the father would he disappear and let her get on with the rest of her life? No, of course not. Renzo might suffer from arrogance and an innate sense of entitlement but he wasn't stupid. She'd been a virgin when she met him and the most enthusiastic of lovers during their time together. He must realise he was the father.

'Of course it's yours,' she snapped. 'And this baby will be growing up with me as its mother, no matter how hard you try to take him away!'

As he put the photo back down with a shaking hand she saw a flash of anger in his eyes. 'Do you really think I would try to take a child away from its mother?'

'How should I know what you would or wouldn't do?' Her voice was really shaking now. 'You're a stranger to me now, Renzo—or maybe you always were. So eager to think badly of someone. So quick to apportion blame.'

'And what conclusion would you have come to,' he demanded, 'if you'd arrived home to find a seedy stranger leaving and a costly piece of jewellery missing?'

'I might have stopped to ask questions before I started accusing.'

'Okay. I'll ask them now. What was he doing there?'

'He turned up out of the blue.' She pushed away a sweat-damp curl which was sticking to her clammy cheek. 'He'd seen a photo of me at the ball. He was the last person I expected or wanted to see.'

'Yet you offered him a beer.'

Because she'd been afraid. Afraid of the damage Drake could inflict if he got to Renzo before she did because she hadn't wanted her golden present to come tumbling down around her ears. But it had come tumbling down anyway, hadn't it?

'I thought he would blackmail me by telling you about my mother,' she said at last, in a low voice. 'Only now you know all my secrets.'

'Do I?' he questioned coolly.

She didn't flinch beneath that quizzical black gaze. She kept her face bland as her old habit for self-preservation kept her lips tightly sealed. He knew her mother had been a drug addict and that was bad enough, but what if she explained how she had funded her habit? Darcy could imagine only too well how that contemptuous look would deepen. Something told her there were things this proud man would find intolerable and her mother's profession was one of them. Who knew how he might try to use it against her?

Suddenly, she realised she would put nothing past him. He had accused her of all kinds of things—including using her virginity as some kind of bartering tool. Why shouldn't she keep secrets from him when he had such a brutal opinion of her?

'Of course you do. I'm the illegitimate daughter of a junkie—how much worse could it be?' She sucked in a deep breath and willed herself to keep her nerve. 'Look, Renzo, I know I'm expecting your baby and it must be the last thing you want but maybe we can work something out to our mutual satisfaction. I don't imagine you'll want anything more to do with me but I shan't make any attempt to stop you from having regular contact with your son. In fact, I'll do everything in my power to accommodate access to him.' She forced a smile. 'Every child should have a father.'

'That's good of you,' he said softly before elevating his dark eyebrows enquiringly. 'So what do you propose we do, Darcy? Perhaps you'd like me to start making regular payments until the baby is born? That way you could give up work and not have to worry.'

Hardly able to believe he was being so acquiescent, Darcy sat up in bed a little, nervously smoothing the thin sheet with her hand. 'That's a very generous offer,' she said cautiously.

'And in the meantime you could look for a nice house to live in for when our son arrives—budget no obstacle, obviously. In the country of your choice—that, too, goes without saying.'

She flashed him an uncertain smile. 'That's... that's unbelievably kind of you, Renzo.'

'And perhaps we could find you a street paved with gold while we're at it? That way you could bypass me completely and simply help yourself to whatever it was you wanted?'

It took a moment or two for her to realise he was being sarcastic but the darkly sardonic look on his face left her in no doubt. 'You were joking,' she said woodenly.

'Yes, I was *joking*,' he bit back. 'Unless you think I'm gullible enough to write you an open cheque so you can go away and bring up my son in whatever chaotic state you choose? Is that your dream scenario? Setting yourself up for life with a rich but absent babyfather?'

'As if,' she returned, her fingers digging into the thin hospital sheet. 'If I had gone looking for a wealthy sperm donor, I'd have chosen someone with a little more heart than you!'

Her words were forceful but as Renzo absorbed her defiant response he noticed that her face had gone as white as the sheet she was clutching. 'I don't want to hurt you, Darcy,' he said, self-reproach suddenly rippling through him.

'Being able to hurt me would imply I cared.' Her mouth barely moved as she spoke. 'And I don't. At least, not about you—only about our baby.'

Her fingers fluttered over the swell of her belly

and Renzo's heart gave a sudden leap as he allowed his gaze to rest on it. 'I am prepared to support you both.' His voice thickened and deepened. 'But on one condition.'

'Let me guess. Sole custody for you, I suppose? With the occasional access visit for me, probably accompanied by some ghastly nanny of your choice?'

'I'm hoping it won't come to that,' he said evenly. 'But I will not have a Sabatini heir growing up illegitimately.' He walked over to the window and stared out at the heavy winter clouds before turning back again. 'This child stands to inherit my empire, but only if he or she bears my name. So yes, I will support you, Darcy—but it will be on my terms. And the first, non-negotiable one is that you marry me.'

She stared at him. 'You have to be out of your mind,' she whispered.

'I was about to say that you have no choice but it seems to me you do. But be warned that if you refuse me and continue to live like this—patently unable to cope and putting our child at risk—I will be on my lawyers so fast you won't believe it. And I will instruct them to do everything in their power to prove you are an unfit mother.'

Darcy shivered as she heard the dark determination in his voice. Because wouldn't that bit be easy? If that situation arose he would start digging around in her past—and what a bonanza of further unsavoury facts he would discover. The drug addict bit was bad enough, but would the courts look favourably on the child of a prostitute without a single qualification to her name, one who was struggling to make ends meet and who had been admitted to hospital with severe exhaustion? Of course they wouldn't. Not when she was up against a world-famous architect with more money than he knew what to do with.

She licked her lips, naked appeal in her eyes. 'And if the marriage is unbearable, what then? If I *do* want a divorce sometime in the future, does that mean you won't give me one?'

He shook his head. 'I'm not going to keep you a prisoner, Darcy—you have my word on that. Perhaps we could surprise ourselves by negotiating a relationship that works. But that isn't something we need to think about today. My priority is to get you out of here and into a more favourable environment, if you agree to my terms.' His gaze swept over her, settling at last on her face so that she was captured by the dark intensity of that look. 'So...do I have your consent? Will you be my wife?'

A hundred reasons to refuse flooded into her mind but at that precise moment Darcy felt her son kicking. The unmistakable shape of a tiny heel skimmed beneath the surface of her belly and a powerful wave of emotion flooded over her. All she wanted was the best for her child, so how could she possibly subject him to a life like the one she had known? A life of uncertainty, with the gnawing sense of hunger. A life spent living on the margins of society with all the dangers that entailed. Secondhand clothes and having to make do. Free meals at school and charity trips to the seaside. Did she want all that for her little boy?
Of course she didn't.

She stared into Renzo's face—at all the unshakable confidence she saw written on his shuttered features. It would be easier if she felt nothing for him but she wasn't self-deluding enough to believe that. She thought how infuriating it was that, despite his arrogance and determination to get his own way, she should still want him. But she did. Her mind might not be willing but her flesh was very weak. Even though he'd wounded her with his words and was blackmailing her into marriage—she couldn't deny the quiver of heat low in her belly whenever he looked at her.

But sex was dangerous. Already she was vulnerable and if she fell into Renzo's arms and let him seduce her, wouldn't that make her weaker still? Once their relationship had been about passion but now it was all about possession and ownership. And power, of course—cold, economic power.

But a heady resolve flooded through her as she reminded herself that she'd coped with situations far worse than this. She'd cowered in cupboards and listened to sounds no child should ever have had to hear. She'd stood in courtrooms where people had talked about her future as if she weren't there, and she'd come through the other side. What was so different this time?

She nodded. 'Yes, Renzo,' she said, with a bland and meaningless smile. 'I will marry you.'

CHAPTER SEVEN

DARCY ALMOST LAUGHED at the pale-faced stranger in the mirror. What would the child she'd once been have thought about the woman whose reflection stared back at her? A woman dressed in clothes which still made her shudder when she thought about the price tag.

Her floaty, cream wedding gown had been purchased from one of Nicoletta's boutiques in Rome and the dress cleverly modified to conceal her baby bump but nonetheless, Darcy still felt like a ship in full sail. Her curls had been tied and tamed by the hairdresser who'd arrived at the Tuscan villa they were renting now that Vallombrosa had been sold, and from which they had been married that very morning. Darcy had wanted to wear normal clothes for her marriage to Renzo, as if to reinforce that it was merely a formality she was being forced to endure, but her prospective husband had put his foot down and insisted that she at least *looked* like a real bride...

'What difference does it make whether I wear a white dress or not?' she'd questioned sulkily.

'The difference is that it will feel more real if you wear white and carry flowers. You are a very beautiful woman, *cara*—and you will make a very beautiful bride.'

But Darcy had not felt at all real as she'd walked downstairs—though she couldn't deny that the dark blaze in Renzo's eyes *had* made her feel briefly beautiful. He had insisted they marry in Italy, presumably on the advice of his lawyers, who seemed to be running the whole show. But that part Darcy didn't mind. A wedding in Italy was bound to be more low-key than a wedding in England, where the press were much more curious and there was the possibility of someone from her past getting wind of it. With all the necessary paperwork in place, they had appeared before the civil registrar in the beautiful medieval town of Barga, with just Gisella and Pasquale as their witnesses. And just four days later they had been legally allowed to wed.

It had been the smallest and most formal of ceremonies in an ancient room with a high, beamed ceiling and although Gisella had voiced a slight wistfulness that they weren't having a religious service, Darcy, for one, was glad. It was bad enough having to go through something you knew was doomed, without having to do so before the eyes of the church.

But there had been a point when her heart had turned over and she'd started wishing it *were* real and that had been when Renzo had smiled at her once they'd been legally declared man and wife—his black eyes crinkling with a smile which had reminded her of the first time she'd met him. With his dark suit echoing the raven hue of his hair he'd made a sensational groom. And when he'd looked at her that way, he'd looked as if he actually *cared*—and she'd had to keep reminding herself that he didn't. It had all been an act for the benefit of those around them. She was here because she carried his child and for no other reason. But it had been difficult to remember that when he'd pulled her into his arms in full view of everyone.

She'd felt so torn right then. Her instinctive response had been to hug him back because that was how she always responded and they hadn't touched one another in any way since he'd turned up at the hospital with his ultimatum of a marriage proposal. But too much had happened for her to ever go back to that easy intimacy. How could she possibly lie in his arms and let him kiss her after all the cruel and bitter things which had been done and said? How could she bear to feel him deep inside her body when he'd been so eager to think badly of her?

She remembered freezing as his hands went to her expanded waist, feeling as if her body had suddenly turned to marble. 'Please, Renzo,' she'd whispered, her words a soft protest, not a plea.

But he hadn't let her go or changed his position. He'd dipped his head and spoke to her in low and rapid English, his fingers spanning the delicate fabric of the dress and increasing the points at which he'd been in contact with her.

'You are dressed to play the part of my bride and therefore you will act the part of my bride,' he'd said softly. 'Let's show the world that I have married a flesh-and-blood woman and not some pale-faced doll.'

It was then that he'd bent his head to claim her lips and it had been the weirdest kiss of her life. At

first her determination had made it easy not to respond, but the sensation of his lips on hers had soon
melted away her reservations and she'd sunk into
that kiss with an eagerness she hadn't been able to
disguise. She'd felt powerless beneath that brief but
thorough exploration. She hadn't been able to hold
back her gasp as she'd felt that first sweet invasion
of his tongue. Heat had flooded over her. Her hands
had reached up to hold on to him as the beat of her
heart had become erratic but suddenly the movement
had become about so much more than support. Suddenly she'd been clinging to him and revelling in the
feel of all that rock-hard flesh beneath her fingertips. She'd wanted him so much that she hadn't even
cared about his triumphant laugh of pleasure as he'd
drawn his lips away because it had felt like for ever
since he'd kissed her and it had tasted as delicious as
having a drink after a dusty walk. Like the first hint
of sweetness on your tongue when you badly needed
the boost of sugar.

A kiss like that was the inevitable forerunner of
intimacy and she must not let it happen again. She
dared not…

'You look miles away.' Renzo's low drawl broke
into Darcy's reverie and she watched his reflected
body as he strolled in from the en-suite bathroom of
their honeymoon suite, wearing nothing but a too-
small white towel slung low over his hips. Crystalline
droplets of water glittered like diamonds in his ebony
hair and, despite knowing she shouldn't be affected
by his near-nakedness, Darcy's brain was refusing to
listen to reason and instead was sending out frantic
messages to her pulse points.

It was the first time she'd seen him in a state of undress since the night of the ball, when they'd come home and he'd made rapturous love to her. The night before Drake had visited and the necklace had disappeared and her whole world had come crashing down around her. A necklace Renzo had been prepared to write off in his eagerness to be rid of her. It all seemed like a dream now and yet suddenly all that honed silken flesh was haunting her with everything she'd been missing.

'So why,' he questioned, his voice growing sultry as he walked over and stood behind her and wound one long finger around an errant curl, 'did you let them put your hair up like that?'

Darcy swallowed because, from this position, far too much of his flesh was on show and his skin was still damp and soap-scented from the shower. 'The hairdresser said loose hair would look untidy.'

'But perhaps your husband doesn't like it to look *tidy*,' he mocked, pulling out one pearl-topped pin quickly followed by another. 'He likes it to look wild and free.'

'Which is slightly ironic given that you're the most precise and ordered man on the planet. And I don't remember giving you permission to do that,' she protested as he continued to remove them.

'I'm your husband now, Darcy. Surely I don't have to ask permission to take your hair down?'

Glad for the tumble of curls concealing the reluctant lust which was making her cheeks grow so pink, Darcy stared down at her lap. 'You're my husband in name only,' she said quietly.

'So you keep saying. But since we're sharing a room and a bed—'

'Yes, I wanted to talk to you about that. Tell me again *why* we're sharing a bed.'

'Because I need to keep an eye on you. I promised the midwife and the doctor.' His black eyes glittered. 'And that being the case—just how long do you think you can hold off from letting me make love to you when you're as jumpy as a scalded cat whenever I come near?'

'I think *making love* a rather inaccurate way to describe what we do,' she said, sighing as the last curl tumbled free and he added the final pearl pin to the neat little line he'd assembled on the dressing table. 'I wish we didn't have this wedding party tonight.'

'I know. You'd much rather be alone with me.'

'I didn't say that.'

'I know you didn't.' His dark gaze was full of mockery. 'But a wedding is a wedding and it is fitting to celebrate such a momentous occasion with friends. We don't want them thinking our union is in name only, do we?'

'Even if it is?'

'Even if it is. So why not try playing your part with enthusiasm? Who knows? Sooner or later you might find the feelings have rubbed off.' He stroked her hair. 'You won't have anything to do, if that's what's worrying you. The food, the wine and the guests have all been taken care of.'

'And in the meantime I'm to be brought down and paraded around in my white dress like a cow in the marketplace?'

He gave a soft laugh. 'Looking at you now, that's

the very last image which springs to mind.' He leaned forward, his hands on her shoulders, his mouth so close that she could feel his warm breath fanning the curls at the back of her neck. And suddenly his voice was urgent. 'Listen to me, Darcy. Neither of us wanted this to happen but it's what we've ended up with. I didn't want to get married and I certainly didn't plan to be a parent and neither, presumably, did you.'

Her lips folded in on themselves. 'No.'

In the reflection of the glass their eyes met and Renzo wondered why, even in the midst of all this unwanted emotional drama, their chemistry should be as powerful as ever. Did she feel it too? She must.

He could see her nipples pushing against the silk of her wedding gown and the darkening of her emerald eyes, but the tight set of her shoulders and her unsmiling lips were telling him quite clearly to stay away. Once he had known her body completely, but not any more. Her bulky shape was unfamiliar now, just as she was. She was spiky, different, wary. It was difficult being around her without being able to touch her and, oh, how he wanted to touch her. That had not changed, despite everything which had happened. Her skin was luminous, her eyes bright, and the rampant red curls even more lustrous than before. Didn't people say that a woman with child developed a glowing beauty all of her own? He'd never really thought about it before now—why would he?—but suddenly he knew exactly what they meant. He noticed the way she kept moving her hand to her growing bump, as if she were in possession of the world's greatest secret.

Pregnant.

His mouth dried. It was still hard for him to get his head around that. To believe that a whole new life was about to begin and he must be responsible for it. He'd meant it when he told her he never wanted a family and not just because he recognised all the potential for pain which a family could bring. He had liked his life the way it was. He liked having to answer to no one except himself. And if every female who'd fallen into his arms had thought they'd be the one to change his mind, they had been wrong. He'd managed to get to the age of thirty-five without having to make any kind of commitment.

Had Darcy done what nobody else had been able to do—and deliberately got herself pregnant? But if that had been the case then he must take his share of the blame. He'd been so blown away by discovering she was a virgin that he couldn't wait for her to go on the pill. He remembered the first time he'd entered her without wearing a condom and the indescribable pleasure he'd felt. It had been primitive, powerful and overwhelming but it hadn't been wise. He had allowed sexual hunger to blind him to reason. He'd allowed her to take sole responsibility for birth control and look what had happened. His heart clenched tightly with an emotion he didn't recognise as he stared into her green eyes.

'Did you mean to get pregnant?' he demanded.

He saw her flinch and compose herself before answering.

'No,' she answered quietly. 'I had some sort of bug just before we went to Tuscany and I didn't realise...'

'That sickness would stop the pill from working?'

'Apparently.'

He raised his eyebrows. 'You weren't warned that could happen?'

'Probably—but with all the excitement about the holiday, I forgot all about it. It wasn't deliberate, Renzo—if that's what you're thinking.' She gave a wry smile. 'No woman in her right mind would want to tie herself to a man with ice for a heart, no matter how rich or well-connected he might be.'

And he believed her. He might wish he didn't but he did. His pale-faced bride in the floaty dress was telling the truth. 'So it seems we have a choice,' he said. 'We can go downstairs to our guests with good grace or I can take you kicking and screaming every inch of the way.'

'I won't embarrass you, if that's what you're worried about. I have no desire to make this any more difficult than it already is.'

'Good.'

Turning away, he dropped the towel and Darcy was treated to the distracting sight of his bare buttocks—each hard globe a paler colour than the dark olive of his back. She could see the hair-roughened power of those thighs and hated the way her stomach automatically turned over when she was doing everything in her power to fight her attraction.

'Tempted?' His voice was full of sensual mockery—as if he had the ability to read her expression even with his back turned. And she mustn't let him realise the accuracy of his taunt. If she wanted to protect herself, she mustn't let him get close to her—not in any way.

'Tempted by what—our wedding feast?' she questioned, sniffing at the air as if trying to detect the rich scents of cooking which had been drifting through the downstairs of the house all morning. 'Absolutely! To be honest, I do have a little of my appetite back. I could eat a horse.'

He gave a low laugh as Darcy scuttled into the bathroom where she spent a long time fiddling with her hair, and when she returned to the bedroom it was to find him dressed in that head-turning way which only Italian men seemed able to pull off. His dark suit emphasised his broad shoulders and powerful physique and he'd left his silk shirt open at the neck to reveal a sexy smattering of dark hair.

Uncertainly, she skimmed her hand down over her dress. 'Won't I look a little overdressed?'

'Undoubtedly,' he said drily. 'But probably not in the way you imagine.'

Her cheeks were still pink by the time they walked into the formal salon, which had been transformed with bridal finery by Gisella and a team of helpers from the nearby village. The cold winter weather meant they couldn't venture out into the huge grounds, but instead enormous fires were blazing and dark greenery festooned the staircases and fireplace. There were white flowers, white ribbons and sugar-dusted bonbons heaped on little glass dishes. A towering *croquembouche* wedding cake took pride of place in the dining room and on a table at the far end of the room—a pile of beautifully wrapped presents which they'd expressly stated they didn't want!

A loud burst of applause reached them as they walked in, along with cries of *'Congratulazioni!'* and *'Ben fatto, Renzo!'* The guests were all Renzo's friends, and although he'd told her he would pay for anyone she wanted to fly out to Tuscany for the celebration, Darcy hadn't taken him up on his offer. Because who could she invite when she'd lived her life a loner—terrified of forming any lasting commitments because of her past and the very real fear of rejection?

But she was pleased to see Nicoletta and not just because the glamourous Italian had helped with her trousseau. She'd realised that Renzo no longer had any lingering feelings about the woman he'd once had a 'thing' with. Darcy might have had an innate lack of self-confidence brought about by years of neglect, but even she couldn't fail to see the way her husband was looking at her tonight—a sentiment echoed by Nicoletta.

'I have never seen Renzo this way before,' she confided as Darcy sucked *limonata* through a straw. 'He can barely tear his eyes away from you.'

Darcy put her glass down. Because he was one of life's winners, that was why. He would want his marriage to succeed in the way that his business had succeeded and because his own parents' marriage had failed. That was why he was suddenly being so nice to her. And that scared her. It made her want to fight her instinctive attraction and to pull away from him. She didn't dare sink into a false state of security which would leave her raw and hurting when their marriage hit the skids. Because it would. Of course it would. How long would it take before her brilliant husband tired of her once reality kicked in? Had he even stopped to consider how a wife at the mercy of fluctuating hormones might fit into his calm and ordered life, let alone all the change which a new baby would bring?

But the evening fared better than she would have imagined. Renzo's obvious appreciation—whether faked or not—seemed to make everyone eager to welcome her into their midst. His friends were daunting, but essentially kind. She met lawyers, bankers and an eminent heart surgeon and although each and every one of them spoke to her in perfect English, she vowed to learn Renzo's native tongue. Because suddenly, she caught a glimpse of what the future could be like if she wasn't careful. Of Renzo and their son speaking a language which the new *mamma* couldn't understand, with her inevitably being cast into the role of outsider.

And that could also be dangerous. Renzo had been reasonable before the marriage, but now she had his ring on her finger there was no longer any need for him to be. If she didn't watch her back she would become irrelevant. She looked around at the elegant room her new husband was renting for what she considered an extortionate amount of money. Could she really envisage their son willingly accompanying her back to an unknown England and an uncertain future if the marriage became unbearable, and leaving all this privilege and beauty behind?

But she ate, chatted and drank her *limonata*, waiting until the last of their guests had gone before following Renzo up to their suite, her heart rattling loudly beneath her ribcage. She undressed in the bathroom, emerging wearing a nightgown Nicoletta had insisted on gifting her. It was an exquisite piece for a new bride to wear and one designed to be removed almost as soon as it had been put on. Despite the hard curve of her baby bump, the ivory silk-satin coated her body as flatteringly as a second skin. Edged with ivory lace, the delicate fabric framed the skin above her engorged breasts and the moment she walked into the bedroom Darcy saw Renzo's eyes darken.

Her own answering tug of lust made her reconsider her decision to distance herself from him, because surely physical intimacy would provide some kind of release and lessen the unmistakable tension which had sprung up between them. But sexual intimacy could also be dangerous, especially in their situation. Something was growing inside her which was part of him and how could she bear to cheapen that by having sex which was nothing but a physical *release*?

She sat down heavily on the side of the bed, not realising that she'd given a little groan until he glanced across at her.

'You must be tired.'

She nodded, suddenly feeling as if all the stuffing had been knocked out of her. 'I am. But I need to talk to you.'

'About…?'

'Stuff.'

His smile was slow, almost wolfish. 'Be a little bit more explicit, Darcy. What kind of stuff?'

She shrugged. 'Where we're going to live. Practicalities. That kind of thing. And we need to decide soon because I won't be allowed to fly once I'm past thirty-six weeks.'

His self-assured shake of his head was tinged with the arrogant sense of certainty which was so much a part of him. 'I have my own jet, Darcy. We can fly when the hell we like, provided we take medical support with us.'

She nodded as she pulled back the covers and got into the king-size bed, rolling over as far as possible until she had commandeered one side of it. 'Whatever,' she said. 'But we still need to discuss it.'

'Just not tonight,' he said, the bed dipping beneath his weight as he joined her. 'You're much too tired. We'll talk in the morning. And—just for the record— if you lie much closer to the edge, you're going to fall off it in the middle of the night and, apart from the obvious danger to yourself, you might just wake me up.' She heard the clatter as he removed his wristwatch and put it on the bedside table. 'Don't worry, Darcy, I'm reading your body language loud and clear and I have no intention of trying to persuade a woman to make love if she has set her mind against it.'

'Something which has never happened to you before, I suppose?' she questioned waspishly.

'As it happens, no,' he drawled. He snapped off the light. 'Usually I have to fight them off.'

Darcy's skin stung with furious heat. It was a lesson to never ask questions unless you were prepared to be stupidly hurt by the answer you might receive. Lying open-eyed in the darkness, almost immediately she heard the sounds of Renzo's deep and steady breathing and fearfully she foresaw a restless night ahead, plagued by troubled thoughts about the future. But to her surprise she felt warm and cosseted in that big bed with a brand-new wedding ring on her finger. And, yes, even a little bit *safe*.

As the keen Tuscan wind howled outside the ancient house Darcy snuggled down into her pillow and, for the first time in a long time, slept soundly.

CHAPTER EIGHT

RENZO INSISTED ON a honcymoon—cutting through
Darcy's automatic protests when she went downstairs the following morning to find him in the throes
of planning it. As she glanced at the road map he'd
spread out on the dining-room table, she told him it
would be hypocritical; he said he didn't care.

'Maybe you're just doing it to make the marriage
look more authentic than it really is,' she observed,
once she had selected a slice of warm bread from the
basket. 'Since we haven't actually consummated it.'

'Maybe I am,' he agreed evenly. 'Or maybe it's
because I want to show you a little of my country
and to see you relax some more. You slept well last
night, Darcy.' His black eyes gleamed but that was the
only reference he made to their chaste wedding night,
though she felt a little flustered as his gaze lingered
on the swell of her breasts for slightly longer than was
necessary. 'And we can consummate it anytime you
like,' he said softly. 'You do realise that, don't you?'

She didn't trust herself to answer, though her burn-
ing cheeks must have given away the fact that the subject was very much on her mind. Sharing a bcd so he
could keep an eye on her was more straightforward

in theory than in practice. Because a bed was a bed, no matter how big it was. And wasn't it true that at one point during the night her foot had encountered one of her new husband's shins and she'd instinctively wanted to rub her toes up and down his leg, before hastily rolling away as if her skin had been scorched?

She told herself their situation was crazy enough but at least she was in full control of her senses— and if she had sex with him, she wouldn't be. And she was afraid. Afraid that the pregnancy was making her prone to waves of vulnerability she was supposed to have left behind. Afraid he would hurt her if he saw through to the darkness at the very core of her. Because something had changed, she recognised that. He was being *gentle* with her in a way he'd never been before. She knew it was because she was carrying his baby but even so... It was intoxicating behaviour coming from such an intrinsically cold man and Darcy might have been bewitched by such a transformation, had she not instinctively mistrusted any type of kindness.

But she couldn't get out of the 'honeymoon' he was planning and perhaps that was a good thing. It would be distracting. There would be things to occupy them other than prowling around their beautiful rented villa like two wary, circling tigers, with her terrified to even meet those brilliantine black eyes for fear he would read the lust in hers and act on it...

So she packed her suitcase with the warm clothes which had also been purchased from Nicoletta's boutique and Renzo loaded it into the back of his sports car. The air was crisp as they drove through the mountains towards Italy's capital, the hills softly green against the ice-blue sky as the powerful car swallowed up the miles. They stopped in a small, hilltop town for an early lunch of truffled pasta followed by *torta della nonna* and afterwards walked through narrow cobbled streets to the viewpoint at the very top, looking down on the landscape below, which was spread out like a chequered tablecloth of green and gold.

Darcy gave a long sigh as her elbows rested on the balustrade and Renzo turned to look at her.

'Like it?' he questioned.

'It's beautiful. So beautiful it seems almost unreal.'

'But there are many beautiful parts of England.'

She shrugged, her eyes fixed on some unseen spot in the distance. 'Not where I grew up. Oh, there were lots of lovely spaces in the surrounding countryside, but unless they're on your doorstep you need funds to access them.'

'Was it awful?' he questioned suddenly.

She didn't answer immediately. 'Yes,' she said, at last.

He heard the sadness in that single word and saw the way her teeth chewed on her bottom lip and he broke the silence which followed with a light touch to her arm. 'Come on. Let's try and get there before it gets dark.'

She fell asleep almost as soon as she got in the car and as Renzo waited in line at a toll gate, he found himself studying that pale face with its upturned freckled nose. Her red curls hung over one shoulder in the loose plait she sometimes wore and he thought that today she looked almost like a teenager, in jeans and a soft grey sweater. Only the bump reminded him that she was nearly twenty-five and soon going to have his baby.

Could they make it work? His leather-gloved fingers gripped the steering wheel as they moved forward. They *had* to make it work. There was no other choice, for he would not replicate his own bleak and fatherless childhood. He realised how little she'd actually told him about her own upbringing, yet, uncharacteristically, she had mentioned it today. And even though that haunted look had come over her face, he had found himself wanting to know more.

Wasn't that his role now, as husband and prospective father—to break the ingrained rules of a lifetime and find out as much about Darcy as possible? And wasn't the best way to do that to tell her something about *him*—the kind of stuff women had quizzed him about over years, to no effect. Because communication was a two-way street, wasn't it? At least, that was what that therapist had told him once. Not that he'd been seeing her professionally. To him she was just a gorgeous brunette he'd been enjoying a very physical relationship with when she'd freaked him out by telling him that she specialised in 'family therapy' and he could confide in her anytime she liked. His mouth thinned. Maybe he should have taken her up on her offer and gathered tips about how to deal with his current situation.

Darcy woke as they drove into the darkening city whose ancient streets were deeply familiar to him from his own childhood. Taking a circuitous route, Renzo found himself enjoying her murmured appreciation of the Campidoglio, the Coliseum and other famous monuments, but he saw her jaw drop in amazement when he stopped outside the sixteenth-century *palazzo* on the Via Condotti, just five minutes from the Spanish Steps.

'This isn't yours?' she questioned faintly, after he'd parked the car and they'd travelled up to the third floor.

'It is now. I bought it a couple of years ago,' he replied, throwing open the double doors into the main salon, with its high ceilings, gilded furniture and matchless views over the ancient city. 'Although the Emperor Napoleon III happened to live here in 1830.'

'Here? Good grief, Renzo.' She stood in the centre of the room, looking around. 'It's gorgeous. Like... well, like something you might see in a book. Why don't you live here? I mean, why London?'

'Because my work is international and I wanted to establish a base in London and the only way to do that properly is to be permanently on-site. I don't come back here as often as I should, but maybe some day.'

'Renzo—'

But he cut her off with a shake of his head. 'I know. You want to talk—but first you should unpack. Get comfortable. We need to think about dinner but first I need to do a little work.'

'Of course,' she said stiffly.

'Come with me and I'll show you where the main bedroom is.'

Down a high-ceilinged corridor she followed him to yet another room which defied expectation. The enormous wooden bed had a huge oil painting on the wall behind it, with elaborate silk drapes on either side, which made it seem as if you were looking out of a window onto mountains and trees. Darcy blinked as she stared at it. *How am I even* here? she wondered as she unwound the soft blue scarf which was knotted around her neck. She looked around the room, taking in the antique furniture, the silken rugs and the price-less artwork. Yet this staggering display of a wealth which many people would covet had little meaning for her. She didn't want *things*—no matter how ex-quisite they were. She wanted something which was much harder to pin down and which she suspected would always elude her.

She showered and changed into a cashmere tunic with leggings, padding barefoot into the salon to see her new husband at his computer, the familiar sight of one of his spectacular designs dominating the screen. But despite her noiseless entrance he must have heard her because he turned round, those dark-rimmed spectacles on his nose giving him that sexy, geeky look which used to make her heart turn over.

Still did, if she was being honest.

'Room to your satisfaction?' he questioned.

'Bit cramped, actually.'

He gave the glimmer of a smile. 'I know. Makes you claustrophobic. Hungry?'

'After that enormous lunch?' She wrinkled her nose. 'Funnily enough, I am.'

'Good.' His gaze roved over her, black eyes gleam-ing as they lingered a little too long. 'Looks like you have some catching up to do. You need to put some meat on those bones.'

She didn't reply to that. She wasn't going to tell him that she felt all breasts and bump. She wanted to tell him not to look at her body any more than was absolutely necessary.

And yet she wanted him to feast his eyes on it all day and make her glow inside.

'We could eat out,' he continued. 'I could take you to Trastevere, where you can eat some real Italian food and not something designed to try to appeal to an international palate. Or...'

She raised her eyebrows questioningly. 'Or?'

'We could order in pizza.'

'Here?'

'Why not?'

She shrugged as she stared through an arch to see a long, softly polished dining table set with tall silver candelabra. 'It seems way too grand.'

'A table is there to be used, Darcy, no matter what you're eating.'

It seemed decadent to find themselves there an hour later sitting on ormolu chairs, eating pizza with their fingers. As if they had broken into a museum and had temporarily set up home for the night.

'Good?' questioned Renzo as she popped the last piece of anchovy in her mouth and licked bright orange oil from her fingers.

'Heaven,' she sighed.

But it still seemed like a dream—as if it were happening to someone else—until they returned to the main salon and he asked her if she wanted mint tea. She didn't know what made her ask if he had hot chocolate and was surprised when he said he'd find out—and even more surprised when he returned a few minutes later with a creamy concoction in a tall mug. A potent memory squeezed at her heart as she took the drink from him—perhaps it was the sweet smell of the chocolate which made the words slip out before she could stop them.

'Wow! I haven't had this since...'

She caught herself on but it was too late.

'Since when?'

She kept her voice airy. 'Oh, nothing to interest you.'

'I'm interested,' he persisted.

She wondered if the shaky way she put the mug down gave away her sudden nerves. 'You've never been interested before.'

'True,' he agreed drily. 'But you're carrying my baby now and maybe I need to understand the mother of my child.'

And Darcy knew she couldn't keep avoiding the issue—just as she knew that to do so would probably intrigue him. Even worse—it might make him start to do his own investigative work and *then* what might he discover? Her heart sank. She knew exactly what he would discover. He would discover the reason for the deep dark shame which still festered inside her. She stared at the cooling chocolate, wishing she could turn back time and that this time he wouldn't ask. But you couldn't turn back time. Just as you couldn't hide everything from a man who was determined to find out.

'It sounds so stupid—'

'Darcy,' he said, and his voice sounded almost *gentle*.

She shrugged. 'The chocolate reminded me of going out to a café when I was a little girl. Going to meet some prospective new foster parents.'

The image came back to her, unbearably sharp and

achingly clear. She remembered strawberry-covered cakes gleaming behind glass frontage and the waitresses with their starched aprons. It had been one of those awkward but hopeful meetings, with Darcy's social worker the referee—observing the interaction between a little girl who badly needed a home and two adults who wanted to give her one. They'd bought her hot chocolate in a glass mug, topped with a hillock of whipped cream and a shiny cherry on top. She'd stared at it for a long time before she could bear to disturb its perfection and when she'd drunk from it at last, the cream had coated her upper lip with a white moustache and made everyone laugh. The laughter was what she remembered most.

'Foster parents?' prompted Renzo, his deep voice dissolving the image.

'I didn't have the most…stable of childhoods. My mother was seventeen when she was orphaned. The roads were icy and her father took the bend too fast. They said he'd been…drinking. The police knocked at her door on Christmas Eve and said she'd better sit down. She once told me that after they'd gone she looked at the Christmas tree and all the presents underneath it. Presents which would never be opened…' Her voice trailed off. It had been a rare moment of insight and clarity from a woman whose life had been lived in pursuit of a constant chemical high. 'And it… Well, it freaked her out.'

'I'm not surprised. Did she have any relatives?'

Darcy shook her head. 'No. Well, there were some on the west coast of Ireland but it was too late for her to get there in time for the holiday. And she couldn't face intruding on someone else's Christmas. Being the spectre at the feast. Being pitied. So she spent the holiday on her own and soon after she went to Manchester with the money she'd inherited from her parents but no real idea about a career. In fact, she had nothing to commend her but her looks and her new-found ability to party.'

'Did she look like you?' he questioned suddenly.

'Yes. At least, at the beginning she did.' Darcy closed her eyes. She'd seen pictures of a feisty-looking redhead with green eyes so like her own. Seen her tentative smile as that young woman cradled the infant Darcy in her arms. She didn't want to tell Renzo what had happened to those looks—not when she couldn't bear to think about it herself. 'Before the drugs took hold. I was first taken into care at the age of two and I stayed there until I was eight, when my mother went to the courts to try to "win" me back, as she put it.'

'And did she succeed?'

'She did. She could put on a good performance when the need arose.'

'And what was that like—being back with her?'

Darcy swallowed. How much could she tell him? How much before a look of disgust crossed his face and he started to worry whether she might have inherited some of her poor mother's addictive traits—or the other, even more unpalatable ones? 'I'll leave that to your imagination,' she said, her voice faltering a little. 'She used me to interact with her dealer, or to answer the door when people she owed money to came knocking. There's nothing quite like a child in an adult's world for throwing things off balance.'

'And were you *safe*?' he demanded.

'I was lucky,' she said simply. 'Lucky that some kind social worker went over and above the call of duty and got me out of there. After that I went to the children's home—and, to be honest, I felt glad to be there.'

Not safe. Never really safe. But *safer*.

'And what did you do when you left there?'

'I came to London. Went to night school and caught up with some of the education I'd missed. It's why I ended up waitressing—nobody really cares if you've got a GCSE in Maths if you can carry a tray of drinks without spilling any.'

There was no sound in the room, other than the ticking of some beautiful freestanding clock which Darcy suspected might have been in place when Napoleon himself was living there.

'So...' His voice was thoughtful now; his black eyes hooded. 'Seeing as so much of your childhood was spent with people making decisions for you, where would *you* like to live when our baby is born, Darcy?'

Not only was it not the reaction she'd been expecting, it was also the most considerate question anyone had ever asked her and Darcy was terrified she was going to start blubbing—an over-the-top response from someone who'd experienced little real kindness in her life. But she needed to keep it together. She'd been given enough false hope in life to build Renzo's offer up into something it wasn't.

'I would prefer to be in England,' she said slowly. 'Italy is very beautiful and I love it here but I feel like a foreigner.' She forced a laugh. 'Probably because I am.'

'My apartment in Belgravia, then?'

She shook her head. 'No. That won't do. I don't really want to go back there.'

He looked faintly surprised, as she supposed anyone might be if their new wife had just rejected a luxury apartment worth millions of pounds. 'Because?'

Should she tell him that she felt as if she'd lived another life there? She'd behaved like someone she no longer recognised—with her balcony bras and her tiny panties. She'd been nothing but his plaything, his always-up-for-it lover who was supposed to have been expendable before all this happened. How could she possibly reconcile that Darcy with the woman she was now and the mother she was preparing to be? How could she bear to keep reminding herself that he'd never planned for her to become a permanent fixture in his life? 'It's not a place for a baby.'

He raised his dark eyebrows. 'You're not suggesting we decamp to that tiny cottage you were renting in Norfolk?'

'Of course not,' she said stiffly. 'I think we both know that wouldn't work. But I would like to bring up the baby away from the city.' She licked her lips and her tongue came away with the salty flavour of capers. 'Somewhere with grass and flowers and a park nearby. Somewhere you can work from, so it doesn't necessarily have to be a long way out of London, just so long as it's *green*.'

He nodded and gave a small smile. 'I think we can manage that.'

'Thank you.'

Hearing her voice tremble, Renzo frowned. 'And you need to get to bed. Now. You look washed out.'

'Yes.' Awkwardly, she rose to her feet and walked across the room, feeling the soft silk of a Persian rug beneath her bare feet. But despite her initial reservations at having told him more than she'd ever told anyone, Darcy was amazed by how much *lighter* she felt. And she was grateful to him, too—stupidly relieved he'd managed to keep his shock and disgust to himself because most people weren't that diplomatic. All she wanted now was to climb into bed and have him put his arms round her and hold her very tight and tell her it was going to be all right. She closed her eyes. Actually, she wanted more than that. Could they be intimate again? Could they? Hadn't that book on pregnancy explained that sex in the latter stages was perfectly acceptable, just as long as you didn't try anything too adventurous?

For the first time in a long time, she felt the faint whisper of hope as she brushed her teeth, her hands wavering as she picked up the exquisite silk nightgown she'd worn on her wedding night, feeling the slippery fabric sliding between her fingers. It was beautiful but it made her feel like someone she wasn't. Or rather, somebody she no longer was. Wouldn't it be better to be less *obvious* if she wanted them relaxed enough to get to know one another again? Shouldn't it be a slow rediscovery rather than a sudden wham-bam, especially given the circumstances in which they found themselves?

Pulling on one of Renzo's T-shirts, which came to halfway down her thighs, she crept beneath the duvet and waited for him to come to bed.

But he didn't.

She tried to block the thoughts which were buzzing in her mind like a mosquito in a darkened room, but some thoughts just wouldn't go away. Because apart from that very public kiss when he'd claimed her as his bride, he hadn't come near her, had he? And something else occurred to her, something which perhaps *she* had been too arrogant to take into account. What if he no longer wanted her? If he no longer desired her as a man was supposed to desire a woman.

Tossing and turning in those fine cotton sheets, she watched the hand of the clock slowly moving. Soon her heart rate overtook the rhythmical ticking. Eleven o'clock. Then twelve. Shortly before one she gave in to the exhaustion which was threatening to crush her and Darcy never knew what time Renzo came to bed that night, because she didn't hear him.

CHAPTER NINE

'So... What do you think? Does it meet with your approval?' Renzo's eyes didn't leave Darcy's profile as they stood in the grounds of the imposing manor house. A seagull heading for the nearby coast gave a squawk as it flew overhead and he could definitely detect the faint tang of salt in the air. A light breeze was ruffling his wife's red curls, making them gleam brightly in the sunshine. How beautiful she looked, he thought—and how utterly unapproachable. And how ironic that the woman he'd spent more time with than anyone else should remain the most enigmatic woman of them all. 'You haven't changed your mind about living here now that it's actually yours?'

Slowly she turned her head and returned his gaze, those glittering emerald eyes filled with emotions he couldn't begin to understand.

'Ours, you mean?' she said. 'Our first marital home.'

He shook his head. 'No. Not mine. I've spoken with my lawyers and the deeds have been made over to you. This is yours, Darcy. Completely yours.'

There was a moment of silence before she frowned and blinked at him. 'But I don't understand. We talked about it in Rome and I thought we'd agreed that a house in England was going to be the best thing for us.' She touched the ever-increasing girth of her belly. 'All of us.'

Was she being deliberately naïve, he wondered—or just exceptionally clever? Did she know she had him twisted up in knots and he didn't have a damned clue how to handle her? Because he was starting to realise that, despite his experience with women, he had no idea how to sustain a long-term relationship. He'd never had to try before. In the past he had always just walked away—usually because boredom had set in and he'd found the increasing demands tedious. But with Darcy he couldn't do that. Furthermore, he didn't want to. He wanted this baby so badly. It scared him just how badly. For a man who'd spent his life building things for other people—someone who considered himself urbane, sophisticated and cool—he hadn't reckoned on the fierce and primitive pride he felt at having created the most precious thing of all.

Life.

But Darcy remained a mystery he couldn't solve. She'd closed herself off to him since that night in Rome. She'd told him more about what he'd already known and the brutal facts had horrified him when he'd thought how tough her childhood must have been. He'd sat up for a long time that night after she'd rushed off to bed, drinking whisky until it had tasted stale in his mouth and gazing into space as he'd wondered how best to deal with the information. But he had dealt with it in the same way he dealt with anything emotional. He'd compartmentalised it. Filed it away, meaning to do something about it sometime but never getting round to it. She'd been asleep by the time he'd slid into bed beside her, her fecund body covered in one of his oversized T-shirts, sending out a silent signal to stay the hell away from her. He remembered waking up to a beautiful Roman morning with the air all clear and blue. They'd gone out for coffee and *cornetti* and he hadn't said a word about her revelations and neither had she. She'd closed herself off from him again and he sensed that he could frighten her away if he didn't let her take this thing at her own pace.

But it hadn't worked.

Because now she looked at him so warily by day, while at night she still wore those infernal all-enveloping T-shirts and lay there quietly, holding her breath—as if daring him to come near. Had he handled it badly? If it had been any other woman he would have pulled her into his arms and kissed her until she was wet and horny—reaching for him eagerly, the way she used to.

But she was not *any other woman*. She was his wife. His pregnant wife. How could he possibly ravish her when she was both bulky and yet impossibly fragile? Her skin looked so delicate—the blue tracery of her veins visible beneath its porcelain fragility—as if to even breathe on her might leave some kind of mark. And against her tiny frame, the baby looked huge—as if what her body had achieved was defying both gravity and logic, something which continued to amaze him. He'd even taken to working solely from home these past weeks, cancelling a trip to New York and another to Paris, terrified she was going to go into labour early even though there were still three weeks to go.

'Let's get inside,' he said abruptly. He unlocked their new front door and stood back to let her pass and their footsteps sounded loud in a house which was still largely empty, save for the few pieces of furniture which had already been delivered. But at least it wasn't cold. Despite the bite of early spring, the estate agent must have put on the heating—knowing that today was their first visit as official owners. The door swung closed behind them and he realised that she was still looking at him with confusion in her eyes.

'Why have you put the house in my name, Renzo? I don't understand.'

'Because you need to have some kind of insurance policy. Somewhere to call home if—'

'If the marriage doesn't work out?'

'That's right.'

She nodded as if she understood at last for her face had whitened, her eyes appearing darkly emerald against her pale skin.

'But you said—'

'I know what I said,' he interrupted. 'But I didn't factor in that the situation might prove more difficult than I'd anticipated.'

'You mean, my company?'

'No, not your *company*,' he negated impatiently, and then suddenly the words came bubbling out of nowhere, even though he hadn't intended to say them. 'I mean the fact that I want you so damned much and you don't seem to want me any more. The fact that you're always just out of reach.'

Shocked, Darcy stared at him. So she *hadn't* been

imagining it. It *had* been lust she'd seen in his eyes and sexual hunger which made his body grow tense whenever she walked in the room. So why hadn't he touched her? Why did he keep coming to bed later and later while keeping their days ultrabusy by whisking her from property to property until at last she'd fallen in love with this East Sussex house which was only eight miles from the sea?

The truth was that he hadn't come near her since that night in Rome, when she'd told him everything about her mother. She felt her stomach clench. Actually, not quite everything—and hadn't she been thankful afterwards that she hadn't blurted out the whole truth? Imagine his reaction if she'd told him *that*, when he was already repulsed by what he knew, even though he'd done his best to hide it. And it was funny how the distance between a couple could grow almost without you realising. They'd been wary in each other's company. As the space between them had increased, she'd found the presence of her Italian husband almost...*forbidding*.

But if she had read it all wrong, then where did that leave her? If he hadn't been making value judgments about her, then why was she being so passive—always waiting for Renzo to make the first move? Yes, he was an alpha man with an instinctive need to dominate but it wasn't beyond the realms of possibility that he was simply being cautious around the baby she carried in her belly. He'd never had a pregnant lover before. He had taught her so much—wasn't this her chance to teach *him* something?

She walked over to him and, without warning, raised herself up on tiptoe to press her lips against his—feeling him jerk with surprise before sliding his arms around her waist to support her. Their tongues met as he instantly deepened the kiss but although Darcy could feel herself begin to melt, she forced herself to pull away.

'No,' she whispered. 'Not here. Not like this. Let's go upstairs. I need to lie down.'

'To bed?'

She took his hand and began to walk towards the stairs. 'Why not? It just happens to be about the only piece of furniture we have.'

An old-fashioned boat bed had been delivered to the master bedroom, her only instruction to the removal men being that the thick plastic covering the mattress should be taken away and disposed of. The wooden-framed structure dominated an otherwise empty room and on its king-size surface lay the embroidered coverlet she'd found when she and Renzo had been rooting around in one of Rome's antiques markets. She hadn't asked for it to be placed there but now it seemed like a sign that this had been meant to happen.

'Get undressed,' she whispered as she pulled off her overcoat and dropped it to the ground.

His eyes were fixed on hers as he removed his jacket, his sweater and trousers. Soon their discarded clothes were mingled in a heap beside the bed and at last Darcy stood in front of him. She was naked and heavily pregnant and feeling more than a little awkward, yet the look of desire in his eyes was melting away any last trace of shyness.

'I feel...bulky,' she said.

'Not bulky,' he corrected, his voice husky. 'Beautiful. Luscious and rounded—like the ripest of fruits about to fall from the tree.'

She shivered as he spoke and he took her into his arms.

'You're cold,' he observed.

She shook her head, still reeling from his words and the way he'd looked at her as he said them. 'No, not cold. Excited.'

'Me, too.' He gave a low laugh as he unfolded the coverlet and shook it out over the mattress.

'It almost looks as if we're planning on a picnic,' she said, her voice suddenly betraying a hint of uncertainty.

'That's exactly what I'm planning. I'm going to feast on you, *mia bella*.' But his face suddenly darkened as he pulled her into his arms and their bare flesh met for the first time in so long. 'I'm out of my depth here, Darcy,' he groaned. 'I've never made love to a pregnant woman before and I'm scared I'm going to hurt you. Tell me what you want me to do.'

'Just kiss me,' she whispered as they sank down onto the mattress. 'And we'll make it up as we go along.'

He kissed her for a long time. Tiny, brushing kisses at first and then deeper ones. And for a while, there were hard kisses which felt almost angry—as if he was punishing her for having kept him away for so long. But his anger soon passed and the kisses became exploratory as he licked his way inside her mouth and they began to play a silent and erotic game of tongues.

And then he started to touch her as Darcy had ached for him to touch her night after lonely night, waiting in vain for him to come to bed. At first he simply skated the palms of his hands down over her, as if discovering all the different contours and curves which had grown since last time they'd been intimate. No area of skin escaped the light whisper of his fingertips and she could feel every nerve ending growing acutely sensitised. Slowly, he circled each breast with his thumb, focussing his attention on each peaking nipple and putting his mouth there to lick luxuriously until she was squirming with frustrated longing. She wanted him to hurry yet she wanted him to take all day. But the rhythmical movements of his hand relaxed her completely, so that she was more than ready for his leisurely exploration of her belly when it came.

Their gazes met as his fingers splayed over the tight drum, his black eyes filled with question. 'This is okay?' he breathed.

'This is more than okay,' she managed, her voice growing unsteady as he slipped his hand down beyond to the silky triangle of hair, fingering her honeyed flesh so that she gasped with pleasure and the scent of her sex filled the air.

She reached for him, her pleasure already so intense that she could barely think straight as she tangled her fingers through his thick black hair, before hungrily reacquainting herself with the hard planes of his body. His shoulders were so broad and powerful; his pecs iron-hard. She loved the smattering of hair which roughened the rocky torso. Her fingertips skated lightly over his chest, feeling the rock-like definition of his abs. She thought his skin felt like oiled silk and she traced a lingering path over the dip of his belly before her fingers curled around the hardness of his erection, but he shook a cautionary head and pulled her hand away.

'It's been too long,' he said unevenly.

'You're telling me!'

'And I need to do it to you right now before I go out of my mind—the only question is, how?'

In answer, Darcy turned onto her side, wiggling her bottom against his groin in blatant invitation. 'Like this, I think.'

'But I can't see you.'

'Doesn't matter. And it never used to bother you. Go on.' She wiggled again and he groaned and she could feel how big he was as his moist tip positioned enticingly against her wet heat. 'You can feel me now and look at me later.'

He gave a low laugh and said something softly profound in Italian as he eased inside her. But the moan he gave was long and Darcy thought she'd never heard such an exultant sound before.

'Okay?' he bit out, holding himself perfectly still.

'More than okay,' she gasped.

'I'm not hurting you?'

'No, Renzo, but you're frustrating the hell out of me.'

His laugh sounded edgy but he began to move. In slow motion, he stroked himself in and out of her, his palms cupping her heavy breasts, his lips on her neck—kissing her through the thick curtain of curls. Darcy closed her eyes as she gave into sensation, forgetting that this was the only time they ever seemed truly equal. Forgetting everything except for the pulse points of pleasure throbbing throughout her body and the inexorable building of her orgasm as Renzo made love to her. Insistent heat pushed towards her. She could feel it coming—as inevitable as a train hurtling along the track—and part of her wanted to keep it at bay, to revel in that sweet expectation for as long as possible. But Renzo was close, as well—she could sense that, too. She'd had him come inside her too many times not to realise when he was near the edge. So she let go. Let pleasure wash over her—wave after sweet wave of it—until his movements suddenly quickened. He thrust into her with a deeper sense of urgency until at last he quivered and jerked and she felt the burst of his seed flooding into her.

Afterwards he lay exactly where he was and so did she. His skin was joined to hers, his body, too. It felt warm and sticky and intimate. Darcy just wanted to savour the moment and her deep sense of contentment as she waited for his verdict on that deeply satisfying interlude. Still remembering the dreamy things he'd murmured when they'd started to make love, part of her anticipating just what his next words might be. But when they came, it felt as if someone had ripped through that lazy contentment like a knife ripping through delicate silk.

'So... Was that my reward, I wonder, *cara mia*?' he questioned softly.

She pulled away from him, aware of the sudden pounding of her heart and the general indignity of turning to face a man when any kind of action was proving laborious. Especially when you were completely naked beneath the gaze of a pair of eyes which looked suddenly distant. She told herself not to read unnecessary stuff into his words—not to always imagine the worst. *He told you he wanted you and that he's been lusting after you...so go with that.*

'I'm afraid I'm not with you,' she said lightly.

'No?' He turned onto his back and yawned. 'You mean that wasn't your way of thanking me for buying you a home of your own? For finally getting the independence you must have craved for all these years?'

Darcy froze as the meaning of his words sank in and suddenly all that vulnerability which was never far from the surface began to rise in a dark unwanted tide. Groping down over the side of the bed, she managed to retrieve her overcoat and slung it over herself to cover her nakedness.

'Let's just get this straight.' Her voice was trembling. 'You think I had sex with you because you made me an overgenerous offer I hadn't actually asked for?'

'I don't know, Darcy.' His tone had changed. It rang out, iron-hard—like the sound of a hammer hitting against a nail. And when he turned his head to look at her, his eyes were icy. Like the black ice you sometimes saw when you were out on the roads in winter. Or didn't see until it was too late. 'I just don't get it with you. Sometimes I think I know you and other times I think I don't know you at all.'

'But aren't all relationships like that?' she questioned, swallowing down her fear. 'Didn't some songwriter say that if our thoughts could be seen, they'd probably put our heads in a guillotine?'

His eyes were narrowed as they studied her. 'And if I promised to grant you leniency, would you give me access to your thoughts right now?'

Darcy didn't react. She could tell him the rest of

her story—and maybe if it had been any other man than Renzo she would have done so. But he had already insulted her by thinking she'd had sex with him just because he'd bought her this house. To him, it all boiled down to a transaction and he didn't really trust himself to believe anything different. He thought of everything in terms of barter between the sexes because he didn't really *like* women, did he? He'd told her that a long time ago. He might want her but he didn't trust her and even though she could try to gain that trust by confessing her biggest secret, surely it was too big a gamble?

'I'm just wondering why you seem determined to wreck what chance we have of happiness,' she said, in a low voice. 'We have a lovely new home and a baby on the way. We're both healthy and we fancy each other like crazy. We've just had amazing sex— can't we just enjoy that?'

Black eyes seared into her for a long moment until eventually he nodded, his hand snaking around her waist and pulling her closer so that she could feel the powerful beat of his heart.

'Okay,' he said as he stroked her hair. 'Let's do that. I'm sorry. I shouldn't have said that. It's just all very new to me and I don't do trust very easily.'

Silently, she nodded, willing the guilt and the tears to go away. All she wanted was to live a decent life with her husband and child. She wanted what she'd never had—was that really too much to ask? She relaxed a little as his hand moved from her hair to her back, his fingertips skating a light path down her spine. Couldn't she be the best kind of wife to him, to demonstrate her commitment through her actions rather than her words?

He leaned over her, black fire blazing as he bent his face close. 'Are you tired?'

She shook her head. 'Not a bit. Why?'

His thumb grazed the surface of her bottom lip and she could feel his body hardening against her as he gave a rueful smile. 'Because I want you again,' hc said.

CHAPTER TEN

DARCY'S FIRST INKLING that something was wrong came on a Monday morning. At first she thought it was nothing—like looking up at the sky and thinking you'd imagined that first heavy drop of rain which heralded the storm.

Renzo was in London unveiling his design for the Tokyo art gallery at a press conference—having left the house at the crack of dawn. He'd asked if she'd wanted to accompany him but she'd opted to stay, and was in the garden pegging out washing when the call came from one of his assistants, asking if she was planning to be at home at lunchtime.

Darcy frowned. It struck her as a rather strange question. Even if she wasn't home, Renzo knew she wouldn't have strayed much further than the local village—or, at a pinch, the nearby seaside town of Brighton. All that stuff they said about pregnant women wanting to nest was completely true and she'd built a domestic idyll here while awaiting the birth of their baby. And hadn't that nesting instinct made her feel as though life was good—or as good as it could be? Even if sometimes she felt guilt clench at her heart unexpectedly, knowing that her husband remained ignorant of her biggest, darkest secret. But why rock the boat by telling him? Why spoil something which was good by making him pity her and perhaps despise her?

Placing the palm of her hand over the tight drum of her belly, she considered his assistant's question. 'Yes, I'm going to be here at lunchtime. Why?'

'Signor Sabatini just asked me to make sure.'

Darcy frowned. 'Is something wrong? Is Renzo around—can I speak to him, please?'

The assistant's voice was smooth but firm. 'I'm afraid that won't be possible. He's in a meeting. He said to tell you he'll be with you soon after noon.'

Darcy replaced the receiver, trying to lose the sudden feeling of apprehension which had crept over her, telling herself it was only because that fractured phone call felt a little like history repeating itself which had made her nervous. At least it hadn't been the same assistant who had stonewalled her attempts to get through to Renzo to tell him she was pregnant. That assistant had suddenly been offered a higher position in a rival company, something which Darcy suspected Renzo had masterminded himself. He'd seemed to want to put the past behind them as much as she did. *So stop imagining trouble where there isn't any.*

But it didn't matter how much she tried to stay positive, she couldn't seem to shake off the growing sense of dread which had taken root inside her. She went inside and put away the remaining clothes pegs—something her billionaire husband often teased her about. He told her that hanging out washing was suburban; she told him she didn't care. She knew he wanted to employ a cleaner and a housekeeper, and to keep a driver on tap instead of driving herself—in the fairly ordinary family car she'd chosen, which wasn't Renzo's usual style at all. The private mid-wife who lived locally and could be called upon at any time had been her only concession to being married to a billionaire.

But she wanted to keep it real, because reality was her only anchor. Despite Renzo's enormous power and wealth, she wanted theirs to be as normal a family as it was possible to be. And despite what she'd said when he'd railroaded her into the marriage, she badly wanted it to work. Not just because of their baby or because of their unhappy childhoods. She looked out the window, where her silk shirt was blowing wildly in the breeze. She wanted it to work because she had realised she loved him.

She swallowed.

She loved him.

It had dawned on her one morning when she'd woken to find him still sleeping beside her. In sleep he looked far less forbidding but no less beautiful. His shadowed features were softened; the sensual lips relaxed. Two dark arcs of eyelashes feathered onto his olive skin and his hair was ruffled from where she'd run her hungry fingers through it sometime dur-ing the night. She remembered the powerful feeling which had welled up inside her as the full force of her feelings had hit her and she wondered how she could have failed to recognise it before.

Of course she loved him. She'd been swept away by him from the moment she'd looked across a crowded nightclub and seen a man who had only had eyes for her. A once-in-a-lifetime man who'd made her feel a once-in-a-lifetime passion, despite the fact that he could be arrogant, tricky and, at times, downright difficult. And if fate—or rather pregnancy—had given her the opportunity to capitalise on those feelings and for passion to evolve into love, then she had to make the most of it. He might not feel the same way about her but she told herself that didn't matter because she had more than enough love to go round. She planned to make herself indispensable—not just as the mother of his child, but as his partner. To concentrate on friendship, respect and passion and reassure herself that maybe it could be enough. And if sometimes she found herself yearning for something more—well, maybe she needed to learn to appreciate what she had and stop chasing fantasy.

She spent the next hour crushing basil leaves and mashing garlic, trying to perfect a pesto sauce as good as the one they'd eaten in Rome on the last evening of their honeymoon. Then she picked a handful of daffodils and put them in a vase and had just sat down with a cup of tea to admire their yellow frilliness, when she heard the front door slam.

'I'm in here!' she called. She looked up to see Renzo framed in the doorway, her smile and words of welcome dying on her lips when she saw the darkness on his face. She put the cup down with a suddenly shaking hand. 'Is something wrong?'

He didn't answer and that only increased her fear. His hands were white-knuckled and a pulse was beating fast at his temple, just below a wayward strand of jet-black hair. She could sense an almost palpable tension about him—as if he was only just clinging on to his temper by a shred.

'Renzo! What's wrong?'

He fixed her with a gaze which was cold and hard. 'You tell me,' he said.

'Renzo, you're scaring me now. What is it? I don't understand.'

'Neither did I.' He gave a harsh and bitter laugh. 'But suddenly I do.'

From his pocket he took out an envelope and slapped it onto the table. It was creased—as if some-body had crushed it in the palm of their hand and then changed their mind and flattened it out again. On the cheap paper Renzo's name had been printed—and whoever had written it had spelt his surname wrong, she noted automatically.

His lip curved. 'It's a letter from your friend.'

'Which *friend*?'

'Shouldn't take you long to work that one out, Darcy. I mean, it isn't like you have a lot of friends, is it?' His mouth twisted. 'I never really understood why before. But suddenly I do.'

She knew then. She'd seen the look often enough in the past not to be able to recognise it. She could feel the stab of pain to her heart and the sickening certainty that her flirtation with a normal life was over.

'What does it say?'

'What do you think it says?'

'I'd like to hear it.' Was she hoping for some sort of reprieve? For someone to be writing to tell him that she'd once told a policewoman a lie—or that she'd missed school for a whole three months while her mother kept her at home? She licked her lips and looked at him. 'Please.'

With another contemptuous twist of his lips he pulled out the lined paper and began to read from it, though something told her he already knew the words by heart.

'"Did you know that Pammie Denton was a whore? Biggest hooker in all of Manchester. Ask your wife about her mam."'

He put the note down. 'It's pointless asking if you recognise the writing, since it's printed in crude capitals, but I imagine Drake Bradley must be the perpetrator and that this is the beginning of some clumsy attempt at blackmail. Don't you agree?' he added coolly.

Her normal reaction would have been to shut right down and say she didn't want to talk about it because that had been the only way she'd been able to cope with the shame in the past, but this was different. Renzo was her husband. He was the father of her unborn baby. She couldn't just brush all the dirty facts under the carpet and hope they would go away.

And maybe it was time to stop running from the truth. To have the courage to be the person she was today, rather than the person forged from the sins of yesterday. Her heart pounded and her mouth grew suddenly dry. To have the courage to tell him what maybe she should have told him a long time ago.

'I'd like to explain,' she said, drawing in a deep breath.

He gave her another unfathomable look as he

opened up the refrigerator and took out a beer and
Darcy blinked at him in consternation because cool
and controlled Renzo Sabatini never drank during
the day.

'Feel free,' he said, flipping the lid and pouring it
into a glass. But he left the drink untouched, putting
it down on the table and leaning against the window
sill as he fixed her with that same cold and flinty
stare. 'Explain away.'

In a way it would have been easier if he'd been
angry. If he'd been hurling accusations at her she
could have met those accusations head-on. She could
have countered his rage with, not exactly *reason*—
but surely some kind of heartfelt appeal, asking him
to put himself in her situation. But this wasn't easy.
Not when he was looking at her like that. It was like
trying to hold a conversation with a piece of stone.

'My mother was a prostitute.'

'I think we've already established that fact and I
think I know how prostitution works,' he said. 'So
what exactly was it you wanted to *explain*, Darcy?'

It was worse than she'd thought because there *was*
anger, only it was quiet and it was brooding and it
was somehow terrifying. Because this was a man she
scarcely recognised. It was as if his body had become
encased in a thick layer of frost. As if liquid ice were
running through his veins instead of blood.

She looked at him, wanting to convey a sense of
what it had been like, trying to cling on to the certainty that there *was* something between her and
Renzo—something which was worth fighting for.
There had to be. He might take his parental responsibilities very seriously but deep down she knew he

wouldn't have married her or contemplated staying with her unless they had *something* in common. 'She was an addict. Well, you know that bit. Only... Well, drugs are expensive—'

'And a woman can always sell her body?' he interposed acidly.

She nodded, knowing this time there was no going back. That she needed to tell him the truth. The cruel, unedited version she'd never even been able to admit to herself before, let alone somebody else.

'She can,' she said. 'Until her looks start to go— and that tends to happen sooner rather than later where addicts are concerned. My mother had once been beautiful but her looks deserted her pretty quickly. Her...her hair fell out and then...'

She flushed with shame as she remembered the kids at school taunting her and she remembered that she'd once thought she would never tell him this bit, but she knew she had to. Because why was she trying to protect her mother's memory, when she had uncaringly gone out and wrecked as many lives as it took to get that hypodermic syringe plunging into her arm?

'Then her teeth,' she whispered, staring down at the fingers which were knotted together in her lap. 'And that was the beginning of the end, because she kept losing her dentures whenever she got stoned. She was still able to get clients—only the standard of client went rapidly downhill, as I'm sure you can imagine, and so did the amount of money she was able to charge.'

And that had been when it had got really scary. When she hadn't wanted to go home from school at night—even though she was so stressed that learning had become impossible. She'd never know what she'd find when she got there—what kind of lowlife would be leering at her mother, but, worse, leering at *her*. That had been where her mistrust of men had started and if that kindly social worker hadn't stepped in, she didn't know what would have happened. To most people, going back to the children's home would have seemed like the end of the road—but to her it had felt like salvation.

'It sounds a nightmare,' he said flatly.

Sensing a sea change in his mood, Darcy looked up but the hope in her heart withered immediately when she saw that his stony expression was unchanged. 'It was. I just want you to understand—'

'No,' he said suddenly, cutting across her words. 'I'm not interested in understanding, Darcy. Not any more. I want you to know that something was destroyed when I received this letter.'

'I realise it was shocking—'

He shook his head. 'No. You're missing the point. I'm not talking about *shocking*. Human behaviour has always been shocking. I'm talking about trust.'

'T-trust?'

'Yes. I can see the bewilderment on your face. Is that word such an alien concept to you?' His mouth twisted. 'I guess it must be. Because I asked you, didn't I, Darcy? I asked you not once, but twice, whether you were keeping anything else from me. I thought we were supposed to be embracing a new openness—an honest environment in which to bring up our child, not one which was tainted by lies.'

She licked her lips. 'But surely you can understand why I didn't tell you?'

'No,' he snapped. 'I can't. I knew about your mother's addiction. Did you expect me to judge you when I found out how she paid for that addiction?'

'Yes,' she said helplessly. 'Of course I did. Because I've been judged by every person who ever knew about it. Being the daughter of Manchester's biggest hooker tends to saddle you with a certain reputation. People used to sneer at me. I could hear them laughing behind my back. And even though my social worker said it was because I was attractive and people would try to bring me down by exploiting my vulnerability, that didn't stop the hurt. It's why I left and came to London. It's why I never was intimate with a man before I met you.'

'Why you never accepted the gifts I tried to give you,' he said slowly.

'Yes!' she answered, desperately searching for a chink in the dark armour which made him look so impenetrable. Searching for the light of understanding in his eyes which might give her hope.

But there was none.

'You do realise, Darcy,' he questioned, 'that I can't live with secrets?'

'But there aren't any—not any more. Now you know everything about me.' Her heart was crashing wildly against her ribcage as she pleaded her case like a prisoner in the dock. 'And I need never lie to you again.'

He shook his head. 'You just don't get it, do you?' he said and his voice sounded tired. 'You knew that my childhood was tainted with secrets and lies. I told you a long time ago that I had trust issues and I meant it. How the hell can I ever trust you again? The truth is that I can't.' He gave a bitter laugh. 'And the even bigger truth is that I don't even want to.'

She was about to accuse him back. To tell him that he'd never trusted her in the first place. Look how he'd reacted when he'd discovered she was pregnant—showering her with suspicious questions when she'd lain in her hospital bed. He'd even thought she'd had wild sex with him just because he'd bought her a house. But her accusations remained unspoken because what was the point? No matter what she did or said, something in him had died—she could tell that from the emptiness in his eyes when he looked at her.

She nodded. 'So what do you want to do?'

He lifted the glass of beer now and drank it down in a draught, before slowly putting the empty glass back down on the table. 'I'm going back to London,' he said and Darcy could hear the bitterness in his tone. 'Because I can't bear to be around you right now.'

'Renzo—'

'No, please. Let's keep this dignified, shall we? Don't let's either of us say anything we might later regret, because we're still going to have to co-parent. We'll obviously need to come to some sort of formal agreement about that but it isn't something we need to discuss right now. I think you know me well enough to know that I won't be unreasonable.'

She nearly broke then—and what made it worse was the sudden crack in his voice as he said those words. As if he was hurting as much as she was. But he wasn't, was he? He couldn't be. Because nobody could possibly share this terrible pain which was searing through her heart and making it feel as if it had exploded into a million little pieces.

'You have the services of the midwife I've employed,' he continued. 'I spoke to her from the car on the way here and explained the circumstances and she has offered to move into the annex if that would make you feel more secure.'

'No, it would not make me feel more secure!' Darcy burst out. 'I don't want a total stranger living here with me.'

He gave a short, sarcastic laugh. 'No. I can't imagine you do. Living with a stranger isn't something I'd particularly recommend.'

And then he turned his back on her and walked out, closing the door with a click behind him. Darcy struggled to her feet to watch him walking down the garden path, past the washing line. The wind was blowing the sleeves of her shirt so that they flapped towards him, as if they were trying to pull him back, and how she wished they could. She considered rushing down the path after him, cumbersome in her late pregnancy, grabbing the sleeve of his handmade Italian suit and begging him to give her another chance. To stay.

But dignity was the one thing she had—maybe the only thing she had left.

So she watched him go. Watched him get into the back of the luxury car with the sunlight glinting off dark hair as blue-black as a raven's wing. His jaw set, he kept his gaze fixed straight ahead, not turning round as the powerful vehicle pulled away. There was no last, lingering look. No opportunity for her eyes to silently beseech him to stay.

The only thing she saw was his forbidding profile as Renzo Sabatini drove out of her life.

CHAPTER ELEVEN

AFTER HE'D GONE, a wave of desolation swept over Darcy—a desolation so bleak that it felt as if she were standing on the seashore in the depths of winter, being buffeted by the lashing sea. As his car disappeared from view she stumbled away from the window, trying to keep her wits about her, telling herself that her baby was her primary focus—her *only* focus—and she needed to protect the innocent life inside her. Briefly she closed her eyes as she thought about what Renzo had just found out—the shameful truth about her mother being a common prostitute. Would she be forced to tell her son about the kind of woman his grandmother had been? Yet surely if there was enough love and trust between her and her little boy, then anything was possible.

She swallowed because nothing seemed certain—not any more. She could understand her husband's anger but it had been impossible to penetrate. It had been a controlled reaction which shouldn't have surprised her—but another aspect of it had and that was what was confusing her. Because he hadn't threatened her with the full force of his wealth and power after making his sordid discovery, had he? Wouldn't another man—a more ruthless man—have pressured her with exposure if she didn't relinquish her role as primary carer to their baby?

Brushing away the sweat which was beading her brow, she knew she ought to sit down but she couldn't stop pacing the room as her jumbled thoughts tried to assemble themselves into something approaching clarity. His voice had been bitter when he'd spoken to her—almost as if he'd been hurt. But Renzo didn't *do* hurt, did he? Just as he didn't do emotion.

Surely he must recognise why she'd kept her terrible secret to herself—why the shame of the past had left her unable to trust anyone, just as *he* had been unable to trust anyone.

But Renzo had trusted *her*, hadn't he?

The thought hit her hard.

How many times had he trusted her?

He'd trusted her to take the pill and, even though that method of birth control had failed, he'd trusted her enough to believe her explanation.

He'd trusted her enough to confide in her when he first took her out to Tuscany and told her things he need never have said. And then, when they'd got back to England, he'd trusted her enough to give her the key to his apartment. He might not have wooed her with words but words were cheap, weren't they? Anyone could say stuff to please a woman and not mean it. But Renzo's actions had demonstrated trust and regard and that was pretty amazing. It might not have been love but it came a pretty close second. And she had blown it.

Tears welled up in her eyes as she stared at the yellow blur of daffodils in the vase. She had blown it by refusing to trust *him*—by not lowering the defences she'd erected all those years ago, when the police had asked her questions and she'd been too frightened to tell the truth, for fear her mother would go to jail. Renzo hadn't judged her because her mother had been an addict and he wouldn't have judged her because she'd been a prostitute—what had made him turn away with that tight-lipped face was the fact that she'd lied to him. Again and again, she'd kept her secrets to herself.

So what was she going to do about it? She looked at the bright blue sky outside, which seemed to mock her. Stay here with the midwife on standby, while she waited for the baby to arrive? Day following day with remorse and regret and the feeling that she'd just thrown away the best thing which had ever happened to her? Or have the courage to go to Renzo. Not to plead or beg but to put her feelings on the line and tell him what she should have told him a long time ago. It might be too late for him to take her back, but surely he could find it in his heart to forgive her?

Picking up the car keys, she went to the garage and manoeuvred the car out on the lane, sucking in lots of deep and calming breaths just as they'd taught her in the prenatal relaxation classes. Because she had a very precious passenger on board and there was no way she should attempt to drive to London if she was going to drive badly.

She let out the clutch and pulled away, thinking that she should have been scared but she'd never felt so strong or so focussed. She kept her mind fixed firmly on the traffic as the country roads gave way to the city and she entered the busy streets of London, glad she was able to follow the robotic instructions of the satnav. But her hands were shaking as eventually she drew up outside the towering skyscraper headquarters of Sabatini International. She left the car by the kerb and walked into the foyer, where a security guard bustled up importantly, barring her way.

'I'm afraid you can't park there, miss.'

'Oh, yes, I can. And it's Mrs, actually—or Signora, if you prefer. My husband owns this building. So if you wouldn't mind?' Giving a tight smile at his goggle-eyed expression, she handed him her car keys. 'Doing something with my car? I'd hate Renzo to get a ticket.'

She was aware of people staring at her as she headed for the penthouse lift but maybe that wasn't surprising. Among the cool and geeky workers milling around, she guessed a heavily pregnant woman with untidy hair would be a bit of a talking point. The elevator zoomed her straight up to the thirty-second floor, where one of Renzo's assistants must have been forewarned because she stood directly in Darcy's path, her fixed smile not quite meeting her eyes.

'Mrs Sabatini.' She inclined her head. 'I can't let you disturb him. I'm afraid your husband is tied up right now.'

Suddenly tempted by a wild impulse to ask whether Renzo had suddenly been converted to the pleasures of bondage, Darcy looked at her and nodded, but she didn't feel anger or irritation. The woman was only doing her job, after all. In the past she might have crumbled—gone scuttling back downstairs with a request that Renzo contact her when he had a free moment. But that was then and this was now. She'd overcome so much in her life. Seen stuff no child should ever see. She'd come through the other side of all that and yet...

Yet she had still let it define her, hadn't she? Instead of shutting the door on the past and walking away from it, she had let it influence her life.

Well, not any more.

'Watch me,' Darcy said as she walked across the carpeted office towards Renzo's office, ignoring the woman's raised voice of protest.

She pushed open the door to see Renzo seated at the top of a long boardroom table with six other people listening to what he was saying, but his words died away the moment he glanced up and saw her. Comically, every head swivelled in her direction but Darcy didn't pay them any attention; she was too busy gazing into the eyes of her husband and finding nothing in their ebony depths but ice. But she was going to be strong. As strong as she knew she could be.

'Darcy,' he said, his eyes narrowing.

'I know this isn't a convenient time,' she said, preempting his dismissal and drawing herself up as tall as she could. 'But I really do need to speak to you, Renzo. So if you people wouldn't mind giving us five, we'll make sure this meeting is rescheduled.'

Almost as if they were being controlled by some unseen puppet master, six heads turned to Renzo for affirmation.

He shrugged. 'You heard what the lady said.'

Darcy's heart was pounding as they all trooped out, shooting her curious looks on their way, but Renzo still hadn't moved. His expression remained completely impassive and only the sudden movement of his fingers as he slammed his pen onto the table gave any indication that he might be angry at her interruption.

'So what are you doing here?' he questioned coolly. 'I thought we'd said everything there is to say.'

She shook her head. 'But we haven't. Or rather, I haven't. You did a lot of talking earlier only I was too shocked and upset to answer.'

'Don't bother,' he said, sounding almost...*bored*. 'I don't want to hear any more of your lies. You want to hold on to your precious secrets, Darcy? Then go right ahead! Or maybe find a man you trust enough to tell the truth.'

She let out a shuddered breath, struggling to get out the words she knew she needed to say. 'I trust you, Renzo. It's taken me this long to dare admit it, but I do. I trust you enough to tell you that I've been scared...and I've been stupid. You see, I couldn't believe someone as good as you could ever be part of my life and I thought...' Her voice stumbled but somehow she kept the tears at bay. 'I thought the only way I could hold on to it was to be the person I thought you'd want me to be. I was terrified that if you knew who I really was, that you would send me away— baby or no baby—'

'You can't—'

'No,' she said fiercely, and now the tears *had* started and she scrubbed them away furiously with the back of her fist. 'Let me finish. I should have celebrated my freedom from the kind of life I'd grown up in. I should have rejoiced that I had found a man who was prepared to care for me, and to care for our baby. I should have realised that it was a pretty big deal for you to tell me stuff about your past and give me a key to your apartment. I should have looked for the meaning behind those gestures instead of being too blind and too scared to dare. And rather than keeping my feelings locked away, I should have told you the biggest secret of all.'

He froze. 'Not another one?'

'Yes,' she whispered. 'The final one—and I'm about to let you in on it. Not because I want something in return or because I'm expecting something back, but because you need to know.' Her voice trembled but she didn't care. This was her chance to put something right but it was also the truth—shining, bold and very certain, no matter the consequences. 'I love you, Renzo. I've loved you from the first moment I saw you, when the thunderbolt hit me, too. Because that feeling never went away. It just grew and grew. When we made love that first time, it was so powerful—it blew me away. I've never wanted to be intimate with a man before you and I know that, if you don't want me, I won't ever find somebody who makes me feel the way you do.'

There was a silence when all Darcy could hear was the fierce pounding of her heart and she could hardly bear to look at him for fear that she might read rejection in his face. But she had to look at him. If she had learned anything it was that she had to face up to the truth, no matter how painful that might be.

'How did you get here?' he demanded.

She blinked at him in confusion. 'I…drove.'

He nodded. 'You parked your car in the middle of the city when you've only recently passed your test?'

'I gave the keys to the security guard.' She licked her lips. 'I told him I was your wife.'

'So you thought you'd just drive up here and burst into my building and disrupt my meeting with a few pretty words and make it all better?'

'I did...' She drew in a deep breath. 'I did what I thought was best.'

'Best for you, you mean?'

'Renzo—'

'No!' he interrupted savagely and now all the coldness had gone—to be replaced with a flickering fire and fury which burned in the depths of his black eyes. 'I don't want this. *Capisci?* I meant what I said, Darcy. I don't want to live this way, wondering what the hell I'm going to find out about you next. Never knowing what you're hiding from me, what secrets you're concealing behind those witchy green eyes.'

She searched his face for some kind of softening but there was none. And who could blame him? She'd known about his trust issues and she'd tested those issues to the limit. Broken them beyond repair so that they lay in shattered ruins between them. The hope which had been building inside her withered and died. Her lips pressed in on themselves but she would not cry. *She would not cry.*

She nodded. 'Then there's nothing more to be said, is there? I'll leave you so that you can get on with your meeting. You're right. I should have rung ahead beforehand, but I was afraid you wouldn't see me. I guess I would have been right.' She swallowed. 'Still, I'm sure we can work something out. The best and most amicable deal for our baby. I'm sure we both want that.' There was a pause as she took one long last look at him, drinking in the carved olive features, the sensual lips and the gleam of his black eyes. 'Goodbye, Renzo. Take…take good care of yourself.'

And then, with her head held very high, she walked out of his office.

Renzo stared at her retreating form, his mind spinning, aware of the door closing before opening again and his assistant rushing in.

'I'm sorry about that, Renzo—'

But he waved an impatient hand of dismissal until the woman left him alone again. He paced the floor space of his vast office, trying to concentrate on his latest project, but all he could think about was the luminous light of Darcy's green eyes and the brimming suggestion of unshed tears. And suddenly he found himself imagining what her life must have been like. How unbearable it must have been. All the sordid things she must have witnessed—and yet she had come through it all, hadn't she? He thought how she'd overcome her humble circumstances and what she had achieved. Not in some majorly high-powered capacity—she'd ended up waitressing rather than sitting on the board of some big company. But she'd done it with integrity. She'd financed her studies and read lots of novels while working two jobs— yet even when she'd been poured into that tight satin cocktail dress she had demonstrated a fierce kind of pride and independence. She'd never wanted to take a single thing from him, had she? She'd refused much more than she'd accepted and it hadn't been an act, had it? It had been genuine. From the heart. A big heart, which she'd been scared to expose for fear that she'd be knocked back, just as she must have been knocked back so many times before.

And he had done that to her. Knocked her back and let her go, right after she'd fiercely declared her love for him.

Her *love* for him.

He was prepared to give up that, along with her beauty and her energy, and for what?

For *what*?

A cold dread iced his skin as swiftly he left his office, passing his assistant's desk without saying a word as he urgently punched the button of the elevator. But the journey down to the basement seemed to take for ever, and Renzo's fist clenched as he glanced at his watch, because surely she would have left by now.

It took a moment for his eyes to focus in the gloomy light of the subterranean car park but he couldn't see her. Only now it wasn't his fist which clenched but his heart—a tight spear of pain which made him feel momentarily winded. What if she'd driven off after his callous rejection and was negotiating the busy roads to Brighton as she made her way back towards an empty house?

Pain and guilt washed over him as his eyes continued to scan the rows of cars and hope withered away inside him. And then he saw her on the other side of the car park in the ridiculously modest vehicle she'd insisted she wanted, in that stubborn way which often infuriated him but more often made his blood sing. He weaved his way through the cars, seeing her white face looking up at him as he placed the palm of his hand against the glass of the windscreen.

'I'm sorry,' he mouthed, but she shook her head.

'Let me in,' he said, but she shook her head again and began putting the key in the ignition with shaking fingers.

He didn't move, but placed his face closer to the window, barely noticing that someone from the IT department had just got out of the lift and was staring at him in open-mouthed disbelief. 'Open the door,' he said loudly. 'Or I'll rip the damned thing off its hinges.'

She must have believed him because the lock clicked and he opened the door and sat in the passenger seat before she could change her mind. 'Darcy,' he said.

'Whatever it is you want to say,' she declared fiercely, 'I don't want to hear it. Not right now.'

She'd been crying. Her face was blotchy and her eyes red-rimmed and he realised that he'd never seen her cry—not once—she, who probably had more reason to cry than any other woman he'd known.

He wanted to take her in his arms. To feel her warmth and her connection. To kiss away those drying tears as their flesh melted against each other as it had done so many times in the past. But touching was cheating—it was avoiding the main issue and he needed to address that. To face up to what else was wrong. Not in her, but in him. Because how could she have ever trusted him completely when he kept so much of himself locked away?

'Just hear me out,' he said, in a low voice. 'And let me tell you what I should have told you a long time ago. Which is that you've transformed my life in every which way. You've made me feel stuff I never thought I'd feel. Stuff I didn't want to feel, because I was scared of what it might do to me, because I'd seen hurt and I'd seen pain in relationships and I didn't want any part of that. Only I've just realised...' He drew in a deep breath and maybe she thought he wasn't going to continue, because her eyes had narrowed.

'Realised what?' she questioned cautiously.

'That the worst pain of all is the pain of not having you in my life. When you walked out of my office just now I got a glimpse of just what that could be like—and it felt like the sun had been blotted from the sky.'

'Very poetic,' she said sarcastically. 'Maybe your next girlfriend will hear it before it's too late.'

She wasn't budging an inch but he respected her for that, too. If it had been anyone else he wouldn't have stayed or persisted or cared. But he was fighting for something here. Something he'd never really thought about in concrete terms before.

His future.

'And there's something else you need to know,' he said softly. 'And before you look at me in that stubborn way, just listen. All those things I did for you, things I've never done for anyone else—why do you think they happened? Because those thunderbolt feelings never left me either, no matter how much I sometimes wished they would. Because I wanted our baby and I wanted you. I like being with you. Being married to you. Waking up to you each morning and kissing you to sleep every night. And I love you,' he finished simply. 'I love you so much, Darcy. Choose what you do or don't believe, but please believe that.'

As she listened to his low declaration of love,

Darcy started to cry. At first it was the trickle of a solitary tear which streaked down her cheek and ended up in a salty drip at the corner of her mouth. She licked it away but then more came, until suddenly they were streaming her face but the crazy thing was that she didn't care.

In the close confines of the car she stared at him through blurry vision and as that vision cleared the dark beauty of his face no longer seemed shuttered. It seemed open and alight with a look she'd always longed to see there, but never thought she would. It was shining from his eyes as a lighthouse shone out to all the nearby ships on the darkest of nights. 'Yes, I believe you,' she whispered. 'And now you need to hold me very tightly—just to convince me I'm not dreaming.'

With a soft and exultant laugh Renzo pulled her into his arms, smoothing away the tangle of curls before bending his head to kiss away the tears which had made her cheeks so wet. She clung to him as their mouths groped blindly together and kissed as they'd never really kissed before. It was passionate and it was emotional—but it was superseded by a feeling so powerful that Darcy's heart felt as if it were going to spill over with joy, until she suddenly jerked away—tossing her head back like a startled horse.

'Oh, I love you, my beautiful little firecracker,' he murmured as she dug her fingers into his arms.

'The feeling is mutual,' she said urgently. 'Only we have to get out of here.'

He frowned. 'You want to go back to Sussex?'

She flinched and closed her eyes as another fierce contraction gripped her and she shook her head. 'I

don't think we're going to make it as far as Sussex.
I know it's another two weeks away, but I think I'm
going into labour.'

It was a quick and easy birth—well, that was what
the cooing midwives told her, though Darcy would
never have described such a seismic experience as
easy. But she had Renzo beside her every step along
the way. Renzo holding her hand and mopping her
brow and whispering things to her in Italian which—
in her more lucid moments—she knew she shouldn't
understand, but somehow she did. Because the words
of love were universal. People could say them and not
mean them. But they could also say them in a foreign
language and you knew—you just *knew*—what they
meant and that they were true.

It was an emotional moment when they put Luca
Lorenzo Sabatini to her breast and he began to suckle
eagerly, gazing up at her with black eyes so like his
daddy's. And when the midwives and the doctor had
all left them, she glanced up into Renzo's face and
saw that his own eyes were unusually bright. She
lifted her hand to the dark shadow of growth at his
unshaven jaw and he met her wondering gaze with
a shrug of his powerful shoulders. Was he *crying*?

'*Scusi,*' he murmured, bending down to drop a
kiss on his son's downy black head before briefly
brushing his lips over Darcy's. 'I'm not going to be a
lot of use to you, am I—if I start letting emotion get
the better of me?'

And Darcy smiled as she shook her head. 'Bring
it on,' she said softly. 'I like seeing my strong and

powerful man reduced to putty by the sight of his newborn baby.'

'It seems as if my son has the same power over me as his mother,' Renzo responded drily. He smoothed back her wild red curls. 'Now. Do you want me to leave and let you get some rest?'

'No way,' she said firmly, shifting across to make space for him, her heart thudding as he manoeuvred his powerful frame onto the narrow hospital bed. And Darcy felt as if she'd never known such joy as when Renzo put his arm around her and hugged her and Luca close. As if she'd spent her life walking along a path—much of the time in darkness—only to emerge into a place full of beautiful light.

'It's not the most comfortable bed in the world, but there's room on it for the three of us. And I want you beside me, Renzo. Here with me and here with Luca.' And that was when her voice cracked with the emotion which had been building up inside her since he'd told her he loved her. 'In fact, we're never going to let you go.'

EPILOGUE

KICKING OFF HER shoes and flopping onto the sofa with a grateful sigh, Darcy frowned as Renzo handed her a slim leather box. 'What's this?' she questioned.

He raised his brows. 'Isn't the whole point of presents that they're supposed to be a surprise?'

'But it isn't my birthday.'

'No,' he said steadily. 'But it's Luca's.'

'Yes.' The box momentarily forgotten, Darcy looked into her husband's ebony eyes and beamed. Hard to believe that their beautiful son had just celebrated his first birthday. A year during which he'd captivated everyone around him with his bright and inquisitive nature, which at times showed more than a glimpse of his mother's natural stubbornness.

Today, with streamers and balloons and a bit too much cake, they'd held a party for all his little friends in Sussex—while the mothers had each sipped a glass of pink champagne. Confident in her husband's love, and freed from the shame of the past, Darcy had started to get to know people—both here in Sussex and in their London house, as well as the beautiful Tuscan villa where they spent as many holidays as they could. Invitations had started to arrive as, for the first time in her life, she'd begun to make friends. Real friends—though her best friend was and always would be her husband. She looked at him now with bemusement.

'Open it,' he said softly.

She unclipped the clasp and stared down at the necklace. A triple row of square-cut emeralds gleamed greenly against the dark velvet and there was a moment of confusion before she lifted her eyes to his. She remembered how, just after Luca's birth, he'd gone to see Drake Bradley and persuaded the blackmailer to tell him where he'd pawned the diamond necklace. He'd got Drake's confession on tape of course and, with the threat of prosecution and prison very real, Renzo had surprised everyone by refusing to turn him in to the police. Instead, he'd given Drake a chance—offering him a job working on the site clearance of one of his new projects in England. Employment Drake had eagerly accepted—possibly his first ever legitimate job and one which, against all the odds, he excelled at. For ever after, he treated Renzo with the dedication and loyalty a badly beaten dog might display towards the man who had rescued him.

Keep your friends close... Renzo had whispered to her on the night when the diamond necklace was back in his possession, after she'd finished remonstrating with him for putting himself in possible danger. But his expression had been rueful as she had held the dazzling diamond neckpiece as if it were an unexploded bomb.

'I guess you wouldn't get a lot of pleasure out of wearing this now?'

Darcy had shaken her head. 'Nope. Too much bad history. And I'm no big fan of diamonds, you know that.'

The next day Renzo had returned the piece to the charity, telling them to auction it again. And he hadn't mentioned jewellery since.

Until now.

'Renzo,' Darcy whispered, her gaze dazzled by the vivid green fire of the emeralds. 'This is too much.'

'No,' he said fiercely. 'It isn't. Not nearly enough. If I bought up the contents of every jewellery shop in the world, it still wouldn't be enough. Because I love you, Darcy. I love what you've given and shown me. How you've made me the man I am today, and I like that man much better than the one I was before.' His voice dipped, his gaze dark as the night as it blazed over her. 'And didn't I always say you should have emeralds to match your eyes?'

Very wet eyes now, she thought, but she nodded as he kissed away her tears. And the jewels were suddenly forgotten because, when it boiled down to it, they were just pretty pieces of stone. The most precious thing Darcy had was her love—for her son and for her husband. And the chance to live her life without shame and without secrets.

'Come here, *mia caro*,' she whispered, practising her ever-increasing Italian vocabulary as she pulled him down onto the sofa next to her.

'What did you have in mind?'

'I just want to show you...' she smiled as her fingertip stroked his cheek until she reached the outline of his sensual mouth, which softened as she edged her own lips towards it '...how very much I love you.'

* * * * *

MILLS & BOON®

MODERN™

POWER, PASSION AND IRRESISTIBLE TEMPTATION

MILLS & BOON®

EXCLUSIVE EXTRACT

Stefano Moretti wants only revenge from his wife, Anna. When she reappears after leaving him, with no memory of their marriage, he realizes that this is his chance…for a red-hot private seduction, followed by a public humiliation! Until Stefano realizes there's something he wants more than vengeance—Anna, back in his bed for good!

Read on for a sneak preview of
ONCE A MORETTI WIFE

Stefano pressed his thumb to her chin and gently stroked it. 'When your memories come back you will know the truth. I will help you find them.'

Her heart thudding, her skin alive with the sensation of his touch, Anna swallowed the moisture that had filled her mouth.

When had she given in to the chemistry that had always been there between them, always pulling her to him? She'd fought against it right from the beginning, having no intention of joining the throng of women Stefano enjoyed such a legendary sex life with. To be fair, she didn't have any evidence of what he actually got up to under the bedsheets; indeed it was something she'd been resolute in *not* thinking about, but the steady flow of glamorous, sexy women in and out of his life had been pretty damning.

When had she gone from liking and hugely admiring

him but with an absolute determination to never get into bed with him, to marrying him overnight? She'd heard of whirlwind marriages before but from employee to wife in twenty-four hours? Her head hurt just trying to wrap itself around it.

Had Stefano looked at her with the same glimmer in his green eyes then as he was now? Had he pressed his lips to hers or had she been the one…?

'How will you help me remember us?' she asked in a whisper.

His thumb moved to caress her cheek and his voice dropped to a murmur. 'I will help you find again the pleasure you had in my bed. I will teach you to become a woman again.'

Mortification suffused her, every part of her anatomy turning red.

I will teach you to be a woman again?

His meaning was clear. He knew she was a virgin.

Anna's virginity was not something she'd ever discussed with anyone. Why would she? Twenty-three-year-old virgins were rarer than the lesser-spotted unicorn. For Stefano to know that…

Dear God, it was *true*.

All the denial she'd been storing up fell away.

She really had married him.

Don't miss
ONCE A MORETTI WIFE
By Michelle Smart

Available April 2017
www.millsandboon.co.uk

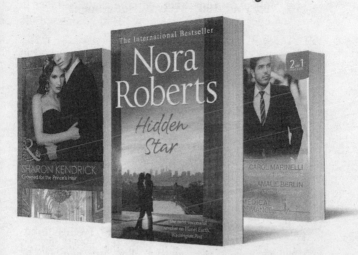

MILLS & BOON®

Congratulations
Carol Marinelli
on your 100th Mills & Boon book!

Read on for an exclusive extract

How did she walk away? Lydia wondered.

How did she go over and kiss that sulky mouth and say goodbye when really she wanted to climb back into bed?

But rather than reveal her thoughts she flicked that internal default switch which had been permanently set to 'polite'.

'Thank you so much for last night.'

'I haven't finished being your tour guide yet.'

He stretched out his arm and held out his hand but Lydia didn't go over. She did not want to let in hope, so she just stood there as Raul spoke.

'It would be remiss of me to let you go home without seeing Venice as it should be seen.'

'Venice?'

'I'm heading there today. Why don't you come with me? Fly home tomorrow instead.'

There was another night between now and then, and Lydia knew that even while he offered her an extension he made it clear there was a cut-off.

Time added on for good behaviour.

And Raul's version of 'good behaviour' was that there would

be no tears or drama as she walked away. Lydia knew that. If she were to accept his offer then she had to remember that.

'I'd like that.' The calm of her voice belied the trembling she felt inside. 'It sounds wonderful.'

'Only if you're sure?' Raul added.

'Of course.'

But how could she be sure of anything now she had set foot in Raul's world?

He made her dizzy.

Disorientated.

Not just her head, but every cell in her body seemed to be spinning as he hauled himself from the bed and unlike Lydia, with her sheet-covered dash to the bathroom, his body was hers to view.

And that blasted default switch was stuck, because Lydia did the right thing and averted her eyes.

Yet he didn't walk past. Instead Raul walked right over to her and stood in front of her.

She could feel the heat—not just from his naked body but her own—and it felt as if her dress might disintegrate.

He put his fingers on her chin, tilted her head so that she met his eyes, and it killed that he did not kiss her, nor drag her back to his bed. Instead he checked again. 'Are you sure?'

'Of course,' Lydia said, and tried to make light of it. 'I never say no to a free trip.'

It was a joke but it put her in an unflattering light. She was about to correct herself, to say that it hadn't come out as she had meant, but then she saw his slight smile and it spelt approval.

A gold-digger he could handle, Lydia realised.

Her emerging feelings for him—perhaps not.

At every turn her world changed, and she fought for a semblance of control. Fought to convince not just Raul but herself that she could handle this.

Don't miss
THE INNOCENT'S SECRET BABY
by Carol Marinelli
OUT NOW

BUY YOUR COPY TODAY
www.millsandboon.co.uk